Elizabeth Bedlam

SUCH TRAGEDIES

Cover by: Elizabeth Bedlam
Formatting by: Elizabeth Bedlam
Editing by: Elizabeth Bedlam and BJ Swann
Published by: SWANN + BEDLAM

THIS IS A WORK OF FICTION.
NO NAMES HAVE BEEN CHANGED, BECAUSE....
The characters are invented & events fabricated.
ALL THOUGHTS AND OPINIONS ARE THAT OF THE CHARACTERS
and should not be mistaken for the author's (who would **NEVER** foist her personal opinions on unsuspecting readers using the guise of a fictional character. That would be wrong.)

READ THIS ★ DESTROY IT ◊ Burn it
CUT IT UP AND TAPE IT TO THE WALLS ...SOAK UP BLOOD ....USE TO BALANCE OUT A PIECE OF UNEVEN FURNITURE....
CONTACT ME OR DONT TO LET ME KNOW HOW IT GOES IF YOU SO DESIRE

Copyleft Ↄ Rights or No WronGs Reserved

Reproduce, photocopy, share....
GIVE TO FRIENDS OR STRANGERS.
Feel free to buy extra copies
to leave around town...
on a bus.... or in a motel room

SWANN BEDLAM
DETROIT | MELBOURNE
INSTAGRAM: @ELIZABETH.BEDLAM @SWANN.BEDLAM
EMAIL: ELIZABETHBEDLAM@GMAIL.COM
WEBSITE: SWANNBEDLAM.COM

PART I: EUSTACE

1.

"You look so grumpy. You always look so grumpy these days. It's making you old." Ada commented, powdering her nose.

"I came, didn't I? Do you really have to go on about this every single time we go to one of these things?" said Eustace. He eyed a young couple walking hand-in-hand towards the community center. He thought they looked stoned. *Hippies.* Eustace was noticing lots and lots of hippies. Their jeans were too tight. The women's blouses were too low for his taste. Long flowing hair and beads all over the place. He bet they smelled like reefer. Eustace wouldn't be surprised if he saw some of his students. "If you insist on dragging me along to these things, I don't get why we can't go out of town. Does the whole community need to know what we do in our free time?"

A young blonde skipped into the community center. Eustace couldn't help but notice she wasn't even wearing a brassiere. What was happening to the youth these days? Didn't they have an ounce of self-respect?

When Eustace was that age he had already taken to wearing a pressed shirt, matching slacks, and polished loafers. If he was home on the weekend, sure, a cardigan would do. Ada was a classy thing back in the day. Eustace remembered seeing her around town, her skirt never above her ankles, certainly never without underwear on.

Now Eustace looked over at his wife. Her face looked as if it'd been gnawed on, the way she puckered her lips and bulged out her eyes. Shallow wrinkles were deepening near her temples like her skin was cracking. There was a time when they'd been unable to keep their hands off each other, but of course that was before her break-down, which in turn led to his (minor) break-down, which was promptly cured by placing Ada in an asylum for a year. None of it would've happened if women didn't have such weak dispositions, Eustace always thought.

"What? What is it *now*?" Ada had known her husband long enough to notice the slight change on his face. He had that look in his eye that said he detested her very presence. Ada always thought if divorce was part of her vocabulary, she would have divorced Eustace after two years of marriage and run off to Paris with that exchange student she knew from university, Leo Blaise. *Oh Leo….*Too bad she was soaked with Catholicism and couldn't even conceive of actually being a divorced woman.

"I just hope none of my students see me at this thing. They'll never take my class seriously again." Eustace rubbed his eyes. He looked in the rear view mirror, his left eye looked a little red. "And I think I've got an eyelash in here, do you see anything?" He pulled his eyelid open for his wife to examine.

"It looks fine. You always think something's wrong," Ada said. "Maybe you should wear your glasses?"

"You sure? It looks kinda bloodshot, doesn't it?" Eustace noticed delicate threads of red stitches moving across the white of his eyeball like a cobweb. He'd been having a string of disturbing dreams this week, maybe that had something to do with it. He was just tired, pure and simple.

"You're a hypochondriac, Eustace. Let's go. I don't want to be the last one in." Ada's voice was flat, unconcerned with his problem. Eustace knew he could have an iron rod running through his eye socket and out the back of his head and she'd say it looked fine.

Her expression showed that he was not getting out of this. Ada tended to drag Eustace to these types of things whenever she developed a new interest (more like a passing obsession.) This tended to happen every six weeks give or take.

A few months ago it was a seminar on UFOs. She was devastated for weeks after that one. "*Why* haven't they visited us?" She kept asking on the way home, over dinner, in between commercial breaks, while she was knitting, while Eustace was trying to read, or before bed.

Eustace wanted to cut off his ears so he wouldn't have to hear her whining about aliens and what was wrong with *her*? Why did ETs visit all these people, but not her? She'd never seen a UFO in her life. It wasn't fair, simply wasn't fair….. But instead of grabbing his wife of twenty plus years and shaking some sense into her, he responded calmly, saying, "Because aliens aren't real, darling."

After that Ada flew into a frenzy, joining a UFO group whose members claimed they were all aliens, and that the mothership was waiting to descend. It was only a matter of time. Thankfully, Ada grew frustrated with the group after one of the leaders died and the mothership failed to appear and beam her corpse into the spacecraft.

Now Ada was swept up in the Eastern spiritualism trend. The Swami Nhincomhpoda, who claimed you could manifest a better, *truer* version of yourself through meditation and visualization, had become Ada's new hobby. She'd bought all three of the swami's books and devoured each one. Despite Eustace's skepticism he was somewhat glad his wife was reading an actual book instead of those insipid women's magazines, even if he thought the entire thing was hippie tree-hugging bullshit.

On the one hand Eustace didn't want children. He thought they were sticky, loud, expensive, and would detract from his work. On the other he wished Ada could have a baby so she'd focus on that instead of all this nonsense.

That's one of the only reasons he could scrape together why he agreed to go to all these things. They'd tried for years to have a child but her body rejected every attempt. Ada was searching for something to fill that void, Eustace understood that. He just wished she'd find something already and leave him out of it.

Maybe this swami would help her manifest some actual interests rather than spending hours on the phone chain-smoking and gossiping or lying around watching daytime TV when she was supposed to be ironing his slacks.

If Ada was at least supportive of his work that would be one thing, but all she ever did was complain that he was gone too much, and that when he was home all he did was sit in his study staring out the window. He was never going to help anyone, she said. He was going to spend his life teaching psychology to college students and that was it! Eustace knew that wasn't true though. He had a real gift for understanding the human psyche; look at how well he dealt with his troubled wife. As much as he wanted to wrap his hands around Ada's neck sometimes and strangle the life from her body, he didn't. He looked after her with care and compassion, accepting the faults in his life partner. If only he could figure out a way to help people develop the same sort of patient understanding not just of others, but themselves.

Many of his students (especially the females) took his class looking for a way to understand themselves. It was less taboo to say you're taking a psychology class than to be seen going to an actual psychologist's office. Most of his university office hours were spent with questions from drop-in students starting with "I'm asking for a friend…"

Then there were the young women and wives who came in to ask a question about an assignment, only to spend the next thirty minutes rambling on about feeling unfilled, repressed, not understanding why they were so underwhelmed with their lives when society told them they should LOVE waxing floors and staring at the walls waiting for their husbands to come home after work. The neurotic female demographic was a self-help gold mine. If only Eustace could figure out a way to tap into it, he'd go right up there with Freud, he just knew it.

"Eustace, stop daydreaming and let's go." Ada rapped her knuckles on the driver side window.

Eustace looked at her. She used to be so sweet that her eyes sparkled, her skin glowed. But after the miscarriages, the breakdown, her stent at Northville Hospital - where she picked up the smoking and TV habit - she'd lost the vigor she once had. She had no interests other than sleeping and whatever seminar she was attending that week. Basket weaving, macrame, pottery, UFOs, diets, yoga, houseplants, bee keeping, cake making, and now, apparently, Eastern thought.

Eustace just prayed she didn't become involved with the Catholics again. There was no way he was spending his Sundays with a bunch of stuffy old church ladies talking about ghosts. *No way.* It took him three years to convince Ada to stop wasting her time, the priest just wanted to get up her skirt. It made his in-laws hate him, but when Eustace and Ada relocated from Berkeley to Lansing he never had to see them, so who cares! The state was mostly Protestant anyway, which made his in-laws weary to even visit.

"I'm coming, Ada. Let me just see to the doors." Eustace reached over and pushed down the lock on Ada's side, before climbing out and locking his own. His keys jangled into his pocket.

"You're such a worry wart, Stash," Ada shook her head, tapping her foot while Eustace straightened his suit.

He'd had to come straight from class to here. He was starving and wanted to unbutton his pants. He could only hope this seminar or whatever it was had cookies.

"You know I don't care for that nickname," Eustace said, taking Ada's hand and helping her up the three stairs, then holding the door open for her.

"What, '*Stash*?' Ha, you love it. It's better than Eustace. Eustace is so old fashioned. It makes you sound old."

"You're only two years younger Ada, not exactly a prize pony these days," Eustace said, following his wife and a few strays into the main community room.

"What did you say?" Ada turned around.

"Nothing, Ada, dear."

"That's what I thought." Ada probably would have dwelled on the comment if she hadn't spotted Joann from down the street.

In a way Eustace blamed Joann for Ada's obsession with these classes. Joann was only twenty-five. They'd met at the staff Christmas party several years back. She had recently married Burt Milton, a middle aged professor and friend of Eustace. Burt taught broadcasting in the AV department. He also helped run the campus public access television station. Eustace didn't know how Joann, young voluptuous Joann, could be attracted to Burt. Eustace hypothesized it had something to do with Burt's family's wealth (he was heir to the Spiffy Mix Baking Company). They moved into a large white colonial at the end of the cul-de-sac, with Joann and Ada becoming fast friends.

Soon after they met, Joann began taking Ada to lectures on art history at the university or Polish cooking classes at the community center. Which was fine - until Burt figured he'd join his lovely young wife and Eustace's insane one.

"Why not make it a couple's thing?" Burt suggested at a barbecue last summer. To which the women agreed. Eustace would just as soon hang himself with his tie, but then he figured if Ada was occupied for at least some of the time, maybe he could simply think without worrying about her falling into hysterics every time she heard another friend had become pregnant. Eustace was secretly worried about what would happen when Joann began pushing out babies, but he'd cross that bridge when he came to it.

Eustace looked around at the community room. All the chairs had been folded and taken out, leaving a large empty space.

"Take a mat?" Eustace heard a voice squeak. It was so timid and soft. It took Eustace a second to realize the question was directed at him.

"A mat?" he scoffed at a tiny bald woman with a wine stain birthmark over her eye. A taller one stood beside her like a pale shadow, both in heavy caftans the shade of honey. "For what? How about just a chair? I'm on my feet all day. Do you really expect me to sit on the floor? After I paid how much? Ten dollars to be here? Unbelievable. Looks like you don't have any cookies either, huh?"

Both females stared at Eustace waiting for him to take the mat.

Upon hearing her husband's uproar Ada rushed over. "Eustace," she said. "You can't meditate in a chair, ha-ha." Eustace found her comment condescending. As if he wasn't hip enough to get it. "Men, right?" Ada patted Eustace on the chest. He looked at her hand forcefully slapping his shirt. "We'll take two mats, please," Ada said.

"Of course. Please, find a space. Swami will be ready to start soon," the taller woman instructed.

"Thank you so much." Ada took two rolled up yellow mats and tucked them under her arm. Both helpers smiled at Ada, but Eustace noticed a long lingering glare from the one with the birthmark. The two locked eyes a moment.

"Sweet lime?" she said after a minute, gesturing to a small card table laid out with tiny paper cups. Ada walked over to pick up two cups, but Eustace wasn't backing down from the little hippie, he continued assessing her, sure she was high on something. The tension only broke when a loud group came in, all chatting excitedly, a few clinging to Swami Nhincomhpoda's latest book, *A Familiar Face.*

"Enjoy," the woman smiled, the other one gave a slight bow. Eustace had no choice but to move on or get trampled by the enthusiastic followers of the swami.

It was discouraging that Eustace had spent his entire career trying to craft some sort of system to reach the masses, to help people like Dr. Freud had. To delve deep into their innermost selves and pull out the trauma. That's what he liked about Freud - the neurologist, and *anti*-psychologist, he put the power of healing right into the patients' hands. They did the hard work, asked themselves the tough questions; the therapist simply acted as a guide of sorts.

Freud helped people discover their deepest wounds. Wounds they might not even realize they had. His methods of psychoanalysis revolutionized mental healing. (Some people - simpletons and amateurs - might *try* to debate that fact, but Eustace always won. "Check and mate!" he'd shout with glee, slamming his fist on the table as the weary so-and-so finally slunk away like a beaten dog.)

Psychoanalysis was a tried and true method for helping people unravel their misery and fully heal. Freud didn't just hand out drugs and shocks like candy while blaming everything else, thus stripping the patient of their power. Eustace was convinced that psychiatry nowadays was simply designed to make money while keeping crazy people crazy. Eustace loathed the modern mental health model, it was appalling. He knew he could do better.

Most psychiatrists and psychologists today were charlatans, relying on trendy theories like Behaviorism. "Oh Please, what useless tripe!!! Radical my ass!" Eustace screamed one evening last summer as he tossed the latest *Psychology Quarterly* into the lake behind his house. Just because the guy taught at Harvard everyone kissed his ass. *Fuck you Skinner, you piece of shit phony!* Eustace thought when he defaced the Harvard doctor's author photo on a dust jacket one time in a bookstore. He slipped the volume back on the shelf, feeling pretty smug about the whole thing.

Yet another empty-eyed woman with pinned empty eyes and no hair took to the stage, sitting just off to the side. People noticed and began to settle.

"Stash, sit down," Ada said, tugging at her husband's wrinkled pant leg. Eustace struggled to get comfortable on the mat which was no more than a thin rectangular piece of cloth. It smelled like an Asian market, dusty and hot. Eustace wondered when was the last time these things were cleaned? He hoped it didn't have bugs on it. The smoky incense someone lit was aggravating his allergies, making it feel as if there were piles of sand dripping from his eye sockets.

"Here, drink this," Ada ordered, forcing one of the little Dixie cups into Eustace's hand. He smelled the drink and recoiled.

"Just drink it," Ada's tone was low and serious. *Do **not** embarrass me,* it said.

Eustace knew if they got in a fight he'd be stuck eating cold leftover chicken for a second night in a row. After this they were supposed to go to Burt's for dinner. Joann always made delicious pot roast with fluffy dinner rolls. His mouth watered thinking about it.

"Fine, fine." Eustace said, tossing the room temperature drink down his throat, grimacing. When he said nothing more Ada looked satisfied and turned her eyes from him to the stage. For a woman with such a short attention span she had razor focus when it came to pointing out her husband's every undesirable trait. Because of this talent, Eustace always thought Ada would have been an excellent mother if nothing else.

The lime drink from the white Dixie cup burned his throat. He wished more than anything for a decent Scotch and some butter cookies. *Thank Christ it was Friday*, Eustace thought. Tomorrow he had an early class, then he was coming home to lock himself in his study to write and drink.

Eustace watched the woman on the stage running a thick wooden striker mallet along the edge of a large brass bowl. What sounded like distorted, strung out bells soon overtook the chattering of the crowd. The ringing of the bowl brought down the energy of the room, making it feel as if the very fabric of reality itself was quivering like a sheet in a breeze.

Eustace found himself gently wavering back and forth as he sat there, hunched forward, arms resting in his lap. The vibrating rings of sound fell over him. *Ripples of water,* his mind told him. Eustace almost felt like he could vibrate his soul out of his body, or step into another reality. There he would be recognized for his genius, put right up there with the greats of Freud and Adler, and sure, even

Jung, why not….

"Stash!" Ada jabbed her sharp little elbow into his ribs, jolting her husband awake.

"Uh, what?" Eustace looked at his wife, who signaled with her eyes to look at the stage. A man draped in heavily-embroidered linen was perched on a pillow in the center of the community room. He had long salt and pepper hair with a red beaded headband. His beard was too long for Eustace's taste. It looked as if the man's face was being eaten by an ungroomed Persian cat. One of his eyelids drooped down, hiding a dead eye. Eustace wondered briefly if he stopped shaving and wore six pounds of jewelry if he'd gain a cult following as well.

After the bowls and humming ceased, Swami Nhincomhpoda sat staring at the crowd for five minutes. The people in the room remained dead silent and as still as that frozen applesauce that came in those little TV dinners Ada liked to buy. It was unnatural, applesauce should be runny, spilling out over the plate, soaking into his chicken…. *Mmmmmm*, more like pudding than an ice cube. Eustace didn't like frozen things, they seemed unnatural. He wished his mother was still alive. Ada was a horrible cook. Why had he ever married such an inept woman? Then he remembered those angora sweaters she used to bounce around in, *oh yeah, he remembered now*…too bad perky breasts don't last.

Eustace felt the weight of the swami's lopsided stare and looked up, locking eyes with the man, who was not much older than him. Was the swami looking at Eustace? The doctor narrowed his eyes and glared back. The swami had a hard gaze as opposed to his hollow-eyed female sidekicks. *Holier than thou.* Maybe Swami could tell Eustace wasn't like all these other desperate shells. He actually had a brain, a tight grip on himself. He bet if he had dinner with Swami Nhincomhpoda the two men would laugh at how weak people's minds were. How sad it was that people had no sense of self and had to turn outward to find fulfillment.

Finally, the swami's steady gaze broke away; he raised his hands in the air and brought them down in a slow, calculated prayer motion. "Seekers of self…" he began, while the audience let out a collective sigh, as if the man's very words lifted their burdens.

Eustace's stomach grumbled, his head pounded, his dry eye throbbed in time with his heartbeat. Why had he ever agreed to come to this? He should have drawn the line at *any* religion, not just that cloak and dagger Catholicism. He was a facts man, not some flake who believed in whatever the hell this guy was rattling on about, spitting and hacking out words as if he had a slippery snake caught in his throat.

"Close your eyes," he heard Ada whisper. He looked over and saw his wife's eyelids open just a slit, looking at him. "Do not embarrass me, Stash," she said once again. Her lips didn't even move. It was as if her warning was coming up from her belly.

The doctor figured he might as well not fight it. Could anyone tell the difference between sleep and meditation? If everyone's eyes were closed they'd never notice if he had a little nap. Then if Ada asked him about his thoughts afterward he'd just state he thought it was all rubbish. Then he'd start talking philosophy, that was sure to put his wife off. It worked every time. He loved watching her eyes glaze over after two seconds, wishing she'd never asked what he thought about this or that.

"Everyone," Swami Nhincomhpoda began in a thick voice that dribbled out into the room. "How can we truly, and I mean *truly* see ourselves when we are blinded by this physical world? Oh, people are so preoccupied with their appearance. Women, you and your hair," (the females in the audience giggled.) "...and men with your muscles," (more giggles, only a little more awkward and uneasy this time.) "But none of that is YOU," Swami Nhincomhpoda emphasized. "You are here and yet… you are not. There are other levels of reality your inner self yearns to connect with. It's only after you open the door that you are able to connect all your spirit fragments, give birth, if you will, to your whole self. The face may be familiar, yes, but that person is unknown to you…. Until now…"

Briefly Eustace cracked his eyelid open. Everyone was smiling and nodding, staring at the nothing inside their own head. He looked over at Ada and her huge grin. He couldn't believe these people were swallowing this load of hogwash. It was all recycled ideas on higher consciousness, a higher awareness of self, all packaged with a neat little bow so desperate folks could swallow it quick and easy without any need to think critically. He wondered - did any of these people actually know what the hell this swami was talking about? Because Eustace began listening only to realize the guy was repeating himself and regurgitating ideas from Huxley to Jung and not really saying anything new.

"...In order to achieve all your goals you must learn to set an intention, take action and you will be able to manifest the desired outcome. Look at me! When I was a tiny little boy living in a mud hut I always told my mother that someday I would live in a mansion. Now I have five mansions all over the world! Each filled with the finest silks and the most beautiful women a man could want! And I don't even have to try anymore. After connecting with my higher self I was reborn!" Swami Nhincomhpoda paused for a moment. Someone coughed; otherwise the room was silent.

"But it all means nothing if you are not fully awake!" Swami began again, "Nothing! You are nothing! Stuff is all nothing, nothing, *NOTHING*!"

Eustace cracked his eyelid once more to see the swami on stage pulling at his gold-threaded garments and clawing at his face.

Christ, how much longer can this mummery go on? Eustace wondered.

"So you ask, how, Swami Nhincomhpoda? How can I do this? How can I be like you? Have a life of mansions and beautiful girls? How can I unite my two selves and manifest all my desires through pure thought alone? That is why you're here, is it not?"

Dead silence. Yes, that was why everyone was there. Why would a person want to spend their life toiling away at a job while trying to better themselves, when there was another way, a *quicker* way, to solve all their problems while sitting on their asses?

Eustace shook his head and let himself drift off. Being a beloved professor was exhausting. Expanding young minds, actually contributing to society was tough but someone had to do it. Otherwise the world would be taken over by fools and phonies like this one.

People would sit around all day wishing they were fitter, smarter, better looking, more ambitious, all the while getting bupkis done because they had to wait to unite with their "spirit" self from some fairy realm.

I can't solve world peace until I reach spiritual enlightenment. I can't afford a bigger house until I'm able to manifest my dream job of being rich simply for existing… Bullshit, thought Eustace. Weak-minded bullshit.

As long as people turned to religion or these wacked out belief systems to solve their problems the world would need people like him to talk sense into these assholes when they had a melt down. No doubt about it.

"…You're in a place. A room, a garden, a hallway. It can look however you desire. This is a place only for you. It is here you shall meet the shadow of your greater self. But for now, you find you are alone. You're walking through the entrance now. Let's take a silent moment to look around the great empty space you've created. Explore the area. Become familiar with your surroundings, for it is a place you will return to again and again. Think of it as a gymnasium for your spiritual muscles."

To amuse himself, Eustace's sleepy mind pictured the hallway at the entrance to the community center. He pulled on the twisted brass handles, opening the double doors, and stepping inside. This was funny, because if anything Eustace wanted to be going out the doors, not coming in. But regardless, he stepped inside the building that in every way looked the same as the real-life community center.

Far off in one of the rooms he heard the vibration of those horrible metallic bowls one of the bald women was playing. The sound started off soft, but then rapidly grew louder before turning to a withered moan, like the wind pushing through a leaky window in November.

The linoleum was the bland color of toasted bread spotted with squares of butter. His loafers squeaked on the highly polished flooring. The walls were the same classy wood paneling.

Eustace walked on down the hallway, noticing it was longer than normal. All the doors to the event rooms were closed as he passed. Eustace walked faster, trying to get to the end. When the room numbers began repeating, the doctor really started to question what was going on here. Hadn't he passed Room 4 a minute ago? How was he back at Room 1?

There must have been drugs in that damn sweet lime drink… God damn it! Eustace grew more annoyed.

As the doctor walked, the dark hallway lit up before him, while the lights turned off behind him, as if they were urging him to continue onwards. Eustace hesitated, looking back towards the entrance. The doors were nothing more than black on black.

A sharp squeak like the swift turning of a shoe caught Eustace's attention. He swung back around, gazing into the darkness ahead of him. There was an oblong shape that appeared to be of a deeper darkness than the rest, like a hole in the midst of outer space.

Eustace remembered the swami's direction: *you find yourself alone…* "But I'm not." His voice sounded too loud in the corridor. "Excuse me, hello?" Eustace went forward, while the darkness retreated backward down the hallway as if shy. The lights clicked on, clicked off, clicked on as he passed under them.

The rooms repeated, (click off) 1 2 3 4 5 6 (click on) 1 2 3 4 5 6 (click off) 1 2 3 4 5 6 (click on) 1 2 3 4 5 6 (click off) 1 2 3 4 5 6 (click on) 1 2 3 4 5 6 (click off) 1 2 3 4 5 6 (click on)

….. "I said hello!" Eustace yelled, angry this person was hiding in the shadows playing tricks on him. Eustace just wanted to take a nap, what kind of mind tricks was this swami playing at? He was supposed to be alone, but no

matter how he tried to force a picture of himself in the empty hallway there was clearly someone here with him.

"Don't be a coward, come out right now!" Eustace
let his voice ring up and down the long space which now
stretched out endlessly before him. A two minute hallway
had grown into oblivion.

The doctor was sure he was catching up to whatever was in front of him. He stopped to catch his breath. It
had been awhile since he'd done any sort of sport. Eustace
was bent over, leaning on his knees for support as he drew
in deep breaths. *Damn I'm outta fucking shape.*

He noticed his soft belly, his heavy chest while his
heart thundered away beneath struggling lungs. Looks
like mowing the lawn once a week in the summer wasn't
enough exercise.

Starting tomorrow Eustace thought maybe he'd
walk to work, he was too young to have a heart attack.
What if he was bedridden? Then he'd be at the mercy
of Ada who would be too busy watching her stories and
talking on the phone to feed him or change his bed linens.
He couldn't even get her to clean the house now. If he was
a vegetable he'd die in his own filth.

Eustace glanced up, his hair normally divided
straight down the middle and plastered down with oil, tumbled forward into his face, with sweat soaking his shirt. He
was no closer to the black hole than when he'd begun.

The figure that had started out like a blob now
looked firmer, more like a man, only… undulating. Once in

a while it seemed to catch a ray of light that didn't have a source. It was as if the thing was taunting him, daring Eustace to come closer.

The doctor wiped the sweat from his brow and moved onward. It was then that he noticed he was back at door number 1. No lights clicked on this time when he put his foot forward into the shadows. The deep blackness didn't retract, instead the void seemed to beckon the confused doctor to enter.

Eustace paused a moment before stepping from the fluorescent strip of light into the pitch. How did he get back to door number 1? And was… Eustace moved forward but the hallway did not. He had reached the end, and the thing, the dark sparkling shape he thought he'd seen, wasn't a hole in space at all.

"A mirror," came the voice from overhead. "Look past the reflection. Look forward not back. Yourself is waiting for you to manifest all your life's wishes. If you do not see them just wait, you will."

It was odd, but the voice was right. When Eustace strained to look further into the dark glass, it didn't reflect the lights or the entrance behind him, but seemed to show the hall that was supposed to be ahead of him. He stood outside door number 1, but in the mirror was reflected door number 2. Eustace could just see the out-of-focus figure… No, not *a* figure, but *his* figure.

From somewhere the urge rose, Eustace had to touch the glass that blurred the future like steam on a windowpane.

The backward figure mimicked Eustace's action, reaching out his arm as if to touch some phantom in front of him. If Eustace was reaching for him, who was his reflection hoping to touch?

As Eustace pressed his fingers on the mirror, he half expected his hand to go through. The face tilted just then, only slightly as if looking off to the side. Eustace glimpsed a smeared profile where his face should have been. He stared harder, willing the figure to appear to him. Knowing there was something else to be seen, like a picture hidden within a picture.

Finally, Eustace was able to make out a sharp circle the deep red hue of deoxygenated blood. That was what glistened in the dark, the endless hole so red Eustace mistook it for black. It turned to look at him now. It was planted in his reflection's face where his eye should have been. A feeling came over him of wanting to fall into that dark ring and come out swathed in the gory wisdom that grew beyond.

The doctor leaned forward, his face almost to the mirror, wanting to fall through. Where this urge stemmed from Eustace couldn't say, didn't even think to question it. He just knew it was this infinite space within his reflection's head that held all the answers, making any question obsolete.

There was no reason to ask *Who? What? Why?* because all the answers laid in there. All his desires, his needs, his true self was down in there, burrowed deep within his own psyche, and yank it out by the roots if necessary

The walls were swept away without warning. The doctor saw himself standing with sand twisting around him like the shape of a broken mother slumped in a door frame. The hot wound of a sun burning overhead.

No sooner did it dawn on him that he was in a desert, than the sun began to fall. Cracking open on impact, blistering the earth in all directions, melting the sand until it turned to glass.

Eustace looked down into the flawless mirror the ground had become. It reflected the fractured sky above. Eustace knew there was more to know. But the voice was telling him to go back. Looking up, Eustace recognized the hands of Blake carving a relief of twisted stars in the sky, and for a second he saw infinity.

Eustace felt that he was being pulled away outside of the mirror land, back to the hall. But still his hand was reaching for that bottomless nothing. He saw the hazy profile of his higher self turning away, taking that knowledge with it down the hall.

Eustace pressed himself against the mirror, needing that part of himself to return. Much to his relief the figure paused at door 6. More a shadow now than a man, but Eustace was sure that it was his true self wearing black tar and raw reds.

The figure moved through the door when the bells

rang a second time, looking more like a ruined Polaroid. The door closed, the hallway continued to shake. *Fuck, fuck,* Eustace screamed in silence pounding on the mirror, wanting to break the damn thing down. Needing to get back into that hole that was dug deep within his other's head, back to the desert of Self.

"Eustace? Eustace? Stash?" The weight of a hand on his shoulder made Eustace jump. He turned his neck so fast he felt a hot pain shoot from between his shoulder blades, running further along the spine, up into his skull as if he were being burned with a hot wire.

"Stash!?"

"Whaaat?" Eustace looked around. He was sitting in the middle of the community room. People were getting up, smiling, looking relaxed, almost high.

"Jesus, are you okay?" Ada looked at her husband's sweat soaked clothes, his flushed face. He looked as if he'd just ran ten miles.

Eustace wiped his brow, taking in several deep gulps of air. It felt as if he were holding his breath and forgot to exhale. His chest burned with the human urge to survive. "Did you…" he took in more air, looking around trying to come to terms with what he'd just experienced, "See that?" Eustace was barely able to get the words out.

"What?" Ada asked.

"Hey there buddy, how did it… What the hell happened to you?" Eustace looked up into the round pork face of Burt and his blue-eyed wife. Both of their smiles wilted

when they realized their friend might be having a heart attack.

"The mirror, in the mirror…and the doors…and…"
Eustace was trying to remember what he saw. The repeating, endless corridor….then the mirror and himself with that
sharp circle cut into his face… a black tunnel… a broken
sky… door 6… He saw himself leave through door 6. But
looking around he remembered that, no, his physical self
was only at door 1.

"Maybe you just need some fresh air," Ada said,
standing and taking her husband's hands in hers. When
Eustace failed to move, Burt stepped in to help.

"There we go, buddy, let's stand up."

"I suppose we can take a raincheck on dinner,"
Joann was saying. Ada answered something in reply as
she and Burt grabbed Eustace's arms, hauling him to his
feet. But Eustace was focused on the stage near the front
of the room. People walked out, the crowd thinning, but the
swami continued to sit as if frozen. Eustace didn't like frozen things…the sight of the man's ruined eye and harry
face unnerved him. Still, Eustace wasn't one to shy away,
he stared right back.

"Aw, dammit," Eustace said, feeling that tight wire
coil up his neck, seeming to wrap itself around his brain
like a tree growing into fence, push itself out through his
eye. He slapped his hand on his face, trying to grab whatever was stabbing him. As if a nerve had sprung free, an
unruly scared snake from a basket.

"Dear?" Ada's voice carried worry.

"Come on buddy, we got you."

"Just get off!" Eustace pushed everyone away. "Something bit me," he said, struggling to stand.

"What?" Joann laughed it off. She was so glad her husband wasn't this embarrassing.

"That's impossible. Maybe you just went a little too deep into the meditation there, buddy. It's supposed to be relaxing."

"What the fuck was that?!" Eustace stumbled forward, yelling at the swami who continued to stare unmoving as Eustace threw his fit. All the images came flooding back through the doctor's mind, as if someone turned on a film strip. *That's* what it was. Not a wire but a movie reel. Up his back, through his head, rushing out his eye and circling back through his guts. He felt it racing through him, making his brain feel as if it were on fire. The images in fast forward, or reverse, he couldn't tell because they moved so quickly everything blurred together and he couldn't make them out.

"Stash!" Ada said, mortified by her husband's outburst.

"There's something… Something in my goddamn eye! I knew there were parasites on those goddamn mats! Or was it the drugs in that goddamn, that *goddamn* sweet lime drink! Fuck!" Eustace headed for the stage. If he went blind or had his brain melt out through his ears,he was holding this witch doctor personally responsible.

Burt took a firm tone, grabbing Eustace's arm when he saw where his friend was heading. "Enough, Eustace. I don't know what you think you're doing, but we're not going to be assaulting anyone today. Now let's go." Eustace glared at Burt before twisting his arm from the man's grip.

"You better hope you don't see my face again," Eustace threatened, thrusting a finger through the crowd towards the guru. He looked around at the worried faces, all staring at him like *he* was lunatic. "You all should throw your clothes away. All this fucking incense or fleas or something…we're probably all infected! I'll probably be blind before the week is over! Fucking filthy hippie woo-woo shit!" Eustace's eye throbbed.

The doctor pushed past a group talking near the doors, the front doors, that were thankfully propped open allowing him to make a hasty exit. That was the last class he was ever going to let Ada and company drag him to. If that meant her going insane and him being an unsupportive husband then fine!

2.

Eustace was brushing his teeth, making sure he didn't have spinach stuck in them. That was what he ended up having for dinner. After the scene at the community center everyone decided it would be better if Ada just took Eustace home. He was probably just stressed and tired.

Ada didn't speak for the entire fifteen minutes it took them to drive home. She hated driving, and focused all her attention on the road. She didn't even want to look at her husband.

Eustace was extremely grateful for her silence, he didn't want to talk about it. His brain had become a giant pin cushion filled with hot needles stabbing into his face. His stomach continued to remind him that he was still hungry, and he didn't get his cookies. Eustace wouldn't be eating any pot roast or fluffy Spiffy mix dinner rolls either.

At home his wife went silently to the kitchen, took the plate of leftover chicken breast from the fridge, and dumped a can of slimy spinach over the whole thing. "Here," she said, thrusting the platter at her husband. "I'm taking a bath."

Eustace watched her go up the stairs, a moment later the door slammed. He looked back down at his cold chicken and canned spinach dinner, taking the whole thing over to the breakfast nook which was used more these days than the actual dining room.

What a waste Eustace thought, looking through the kitchen into the empty room beyond. It held the overpriced mahogany dining room table Ada insisted they needed when they moved in here over a decade ago. She'd thought the seats would be filled with children, family, and guests. Lavish dinners and Christmas meals, social functions. But the carved wood only continued to gather dust. No matter how many cocktail parties Ada threw, the seats were always empty at the end of the day.

Eustace turned away and looked out the window at the lake, it was calm tonight. The waters were probably still cold, but as summer came on he looked forward to fishing again. Pulling the Bluegill and Largemouth Bass from warm water, beating them to death on the side of his boat, pulling the guts out and grilling them up. Nothing tasted better than something you killed with your own hands, Eustace thought. Weird, he couldn't say where that thought came from.

Looking down at his chicken and soggy spinach that Ada had failed to drain properly, he was disgusted, shoving the food away, his appetite ruined. An urge to fish, hunt, and use his hands blossomed inside him. The feeling was a bud so small he hardly felt it, but knew somewhere in the dark it was putting down roots.

+++

After rinsing his toothbrush, Eustace caught a glimpse of himself in the mirror. The sclera of his eye, normally a healthy white, resembled more a seedy strawberry than a healthy eyeball. He almost thought the lid seemed swollen too, like an allergic reaction. *Probably all those stinky woohoo sticks,* he thought, poking at it with the blunt tip of his finger.

There was pressure when he touched it, as if it might burst with eggs. Maybe something got inside there and made a nest. It was only a matter of time before the babies hatched. A parasitic wasp came to mind. Last summer Eustace recalled seeing them flying around wondering what the hell is that giant thing? Only to find it was planting eggs into the backs of the tomato worms in the garden.

At first seeing the white pill shaped things on the back of the green hornworms disturbed Eustace. But then, knowing eventually that those larvae would hatch and devour the bastards chomping on his prized Beefsteak tomatoes, made him chuckle with glee. *What goes around comes around,* he sang to himself, while tossing one of the worms he found without the white eggs into the bonfire he had nearby. It snapped and exploded in the heat, making Eustace reflect on how much he loved vegetable gardening.

The doctor blinked, rotating his eyeball, his vision was a little fuzzy, but that was nothing new. Maybe he should start wearing his glasses like Ada said. He wasn't a spring chicken, but he wasn't old either. Eustace thought about his glasses, he supposed they did make him look distinguished. He had a picture of Freud in his study. In it the man wore round glasses. Eustace had gotten a pair to match a few years ago. Perhaps he was straining and didn't realize it, that's where this migraine was coming from.

"Hell if I know," Eustace mumbled to his unresponsive reflection. He flushed his eyes with water, then made a mental note to wear his glasses tomorrow. Judging from the slight bulge in his middle, he should probably cut down on the sweets as well. That shouldn't be too hard, considering whenever Ada was inspired to make anything it tended to taste like wet flour paste doused in maple syrup. If on the rare occasion she bought pastry from the bakery or chocolates from the sweet shop, she had an annoying habit of taking a bite out of each one. The ones she liked she ate during the afternoon while Eustace was at work. The ones she didn't care for she put them uncovered into the refrigerator. By the time Eustace arrived home they were dried out.

A few times in a desperate attempt for a little treat with his nightcap he took out a Danish or slice of pie, thinking maybe he could eat around Ada's bite mark. But the pie crust would be soggy on the bottom, the frosting dry, or fruit middle of the Danish crusted. Eustace would dump the rest of the plate into the trash bin under the sink. *What bullshit,* he'd think, refilling his whiskey glass, thankful Ada only drank women's cocktails like white Russians and mint juleps and left his Wild Turkey alone.

"Turn out the light," Ada murmured when Eustace came to bed. She rolled on her side so Eustace only saw a head of hair rollers covered with blue netting, reminding him of a frosted spider web. At least Ada wasn't wearing the green gunk on her face tonight. It was supposed to make her look younger just like corsets were supposed to make a woman look slimmer. Eustace didn't get it. He told Ada it simply made her look like a swamp beast, which she didn't find amusing.

Eustace settled down beneath the covers, staring up at the bumpy stucco ceiling. He was tired. It was a long day, with morning and afternoon classes teeming with bored faces and stupid questions, followed by the community center mess that Eustace would rather forget about. He was painfully aware that only a few feet away sitting on Ada's nightstand was Swami Nhincomhpoda's *Familiar Face* book. The idea made his eye throb and his skin feel clammy, despite the warm evening.

Gently, so as not to disturb Ada, he sat up and looked over at the stack of books on the nightstand. There was a pen nearby which his wife used to underline and write notes. The cover showed a face divided up into prisms streaked with light. On the back cover Eustace knew was a large black and white photo of the swami looking like a jerk.

"Stash? What are you doing?" Ada, half asleep,

looked over her shoulder at her husband. "Why are you just sitting there? What's wrong?" she asked.

Eustace didn't realize he'd been staring. "Nothing, go back to sleep, Ada. I was just thinking about the swami..." Eustace laid down again, looking back up at the peaks and craters of the ceiling.

"Swami Nhincomhpoda? Why?" Ada asked.

"My eye hurts. Go to sleep."

Ada mumbled, "Good night," turning away, soon she was wheezing.

It was an hour before Eustace finally felt his mind becoming weary. He didn't want to admit it but he was a little apprehensive to sleep, so perhaps it was his nerves keeping him awake. He kept seeing that underdeveloped reflection of himself, that stark hole in his face, with all the knowledge settled down at the bottom.

It felt like all the answers he was seeking in his life were there, in the broken little pieces laying at the bottom of his brain, floating in goo, sticking to the sides like egg shells that had fallen into the mixing bowl with the yolk.

There was a natural urge to stick your finger in and fish them out, but they were slippery. Just when you thought you trapped the sucker, the chip would slide off into the egg white leaving you to wonder if you should just eat the damn egg, knowing that the little crunch you felt between your molars could be shell or pepper. What could it hurt? Or should you continue to pursue the fragment with fingernail, fork, and spoon even at the expense of your own sanity?

Damn it, Eustace noticed he was back in the community room hallway. It was a strange thing to feel yourself in a dream, to know it was a dream, yet feel in your bones it meant something more. Eustace walked quickly from shadow to light, doors 1-6 passed then passed again. The fluorescent bulbs buzzed and died, highlighting his path. When the twisting glimmer caught his attention, his steps slowed till he was standing in front of the long unadorned mirror bolted to the wall.

"Hello," he said, waiting for his reflection to turn and acknowledge him. He wanted to see that empty space, so rich and red it appeared black in places, *like blood under the moon.* "What is this? Hey?!" Eustace rapped his fist on the mirror, trying to get the attention of the shadow he felt was ignoring him.

It was like yelling at smoke. But slowly the figure filled in like grains of sand coming together till the thing looked as solid as Eustace.

The doctor had to fight the urge not to look beside him because he knew despite what he saw in the mirror nothing was there. But perhaps the problem lay not in the figure but in the mirror itself. The sheet of black glass was something more, allowing him to peer past his physical self and connect to his own higher consciousness.

The idea washed over Eustace, and as mad as it sounded, it was the only thing that felt right. Eustace bent forward, holding the side of his face, feeling the pressure of unseen hands pushing along the insides, causing his head to feel swollen as if he'd been stung. He was just waiting for his eye to pop out and roll onto the ground.

Hello, came a word through the curtain of darkness. Eustace's eyes rolled up. The figure posing as his reflection was nearly in focus now, standing closer to the mirror this time. It was him, Eustace, only… *better*. His hair was combed back, he was shaved clean, his clothing pressed. Eustace couldn't say how long he stared back at that face of his, knowing his dumb expression didn't match the calm, confident look that sat on the other's lips. Eustace touched his inflamed eye. The other's actions were delayed, but it finally reached up and touched the empty space where its eye was supposed to grow.

The need for Eustace to push his thumb into his own socket came out of nowhere, but nonetheless, it existed. He knew it would hurt but there was something planted back there that needed light to grow. *Intention…* the thought was there in his mind, though neither he nor the other spoke it.

Intention.

Eustace let the word melt on his tongue, his thumb still lingering at the corner of his eye, as if ready to pop the pupil at any moment.

"Intention…" he got the nerve to say the word out loud, noticing his lips were moving but his reflection's was not. He said it as if it were foreign, a word he had never heard or used till today. *In-ten-tion.*

What was the intention behind bursting his eye? It had always been there. What was the rush to rid himself of it now? Sure, it throbbed, it was dry, plus black speckles had emerged as if the thing were moldy and past its expiration date, but….was that what he really wanted to do right now?

Eustace leaned closer to his other self, the self he wished to be. Clever, slim, suave, confident, cunning like a predator. Right now he felt lumpy, clumsy, like an angry schmuck most of the time. Even his wife thought he was a failure and an embarrassment. He couldn't even get a job teaching at an Ivy League university, but had to settle for a second-rate one in Michigan no less. He couldn't even make it to the grand lecture halls of the east coast, and forget about Europe. Oxford was beyond his reach, even he knew that.

Then hands, black as if covered with coal dust, came up to the mirror and pushed through the glass as if it were merely water. Eustace felt for the first time real fear when the thing's fingers grazed him. It's face passing through the glass, now too close. It's breath powdery and dry, a furnace blowing in his mouth. Was this what he wanted? Eustace closed his eyes, feeling he was about to be consumed.

The breath was awful, rotten fruit and old socks awful. "Stash, you'll be late." Eustace looked straight up into Ada's face. She was blocking the view of the stucco ceiling. Soon the doctor took note of his sore muscles. His fists were clenched at his sides. He was lying rail straight as if sleeping on a board. He felt as if he were bracing for something.

"Jesus, Ada, brush your damn teeth." Eustace sat up, moving her away.

"Next time you can be late then," she said, throwing back the blankets.

"Fuck, what a nightmare," Eustace said. Even he was unsure if the remark was in regards to his dream or his wife, maybe both. He blinked, one eye felt watery, the other dry as if the tear duct had stopped working, A hard bump had mushroomed near the corner of the lid, *a sty, how annoying*. That made Eustace feel a little better. It was all just a dream, left over trauma from that damn swami and his hippie jamboree. It was only natural that it would haunt his sleep. As for the pressure in his eye, of course there was a natural explanation. Some dirt got stuck in a pore of his eyelid, it would clear up in a day or so. He'd just put a tea bag on it like his mother had taught him. Eustace had other things to think about today.

Despite his throbbing eye and his rude awakening the doctor felt oddly good. Almost better than good, optimistic and energized, despite his trouble getting to bed last night and that dream.

There was an eerie feeling he couldn't quite put his finger on, as if he were being watched while sleeping. As he was standing in the corridor of the community room, his other self from the mirror was standing in his bedroom observing him.

Eustace tried to shake it off, focusing on this new bout of optimism. He realized maybe he'd fallen into a rut, and yesterday was a cumulation of it all. His unconscious mind was telling him to break out of his routine and try something new. *God damn right,* Eustace thought while he combed his hair. Instead of dividing it down like the center like usual, he oiled it and slicked it straight back. He couldn't believe how it opened up his face. For a mid-forties man, he was looking pretty good if he did say so himself.

In his closet he pulled out the set of wool onyx trousers he normally saved for funerals and Christmas. They were tailored and fit perfectly. Eustace wondered briefly why he wore anything other than tailored suits. He noticed he felt better when things fit well. He buttoned his shirt, and decided fuck it, he wasn't going to wear a tie today and left the top button of his white shirt open. It was spring, soon to be summer, why not be a little adventurous?

Stopping by his dresser he took his underused glasses from the top drawer. "Perfect," he said, looking at himself in the mirror on his wife's vanity table.

Ada noted the changes in her husband's appearance straight away when Eustace strutted into the kitchen. "Glad you took my advice," she said, setting coffee and burnt toast down in front of him. Normally the thought of bitter coffee and blackened bread would depress Eustace, but he didn't have to eat it!

"Why do you say that dear?" he asked, pushing the plate aside and opening the newspaper.

"Well, you're wearing your glasses for one, and two, because you actually look… *nice*," she said, as if she couldn't believe her husband was still an attractive man.

Eustace gave her a passive smile and snapped open the business section of the *Lansing State Journal.* "Maybe Swami Nhincomhpoda can even help you," Ada said, sitting down, reaching for the Lifestyle section.

Eustace grabbed her wrist across the table making his wife jump. She looked at him with an expression of pure shock. He'd never touched her so forcefully before. "I don't want to hear anymore about the hippie bullshit of Swami Shitstain. That's one of those cults you always hear about, and I don't want you involved. If you need enlightenment I'll get you some mescaline like all the great thinkers, understand me?" he said in a dead tone.

Ada's eyes locked with his unflinching gaze a moment before he released her, going back to his paper as if nothing had happened. Ada swallowed, waiting a second before quickly picking up her newspaper section and retreating to the other side of the table. She couldn't help but notice the red ring forming around her wrist.

Neither husband nor wife talked till Eustace took his blazer off the coat hanger. "You're leaving already? Your class doesn't start for an hour." Ada said, standing in the doorway. Eustace looked at the pathetic creature, still in her blue bathrobe with curlers. She'd probably look like that when he came home.

"I'm walking today, Ada. And some things are going to change around here."

"Oh, are they?" she asked, wondering what the hell her husband was going on about. When did he get so high and mighty?

Eustace buttoned his tweed blazer, then smoothed his hair in the mirror by the door. For a second he thought he saw himself standing in the doorway, that fuzzy out-of-focus blob from his dream. Startled, he turned quickly only to see Ada still leaning there, her lips puckered as if she were a spoiled child. "Yes, they are," Eustace told her. The woman obviously needed direction. Maybe she was like this because he wasn't firm enough with her, letting her get mixed up with bohemians like Joann and filling her head with nonsensical books from that tea room/book store near campus. He had to lay down some ground rules, that much as obvious.

"I want you to get dressed and go grocery shopping this morning. For my dinner I want a steak, a baked potato with sour cream, and pick up a box of that Spiffy dinner roll mix. The extra fluffy kind like Joann makes. Got it?" He saw Ada's eyebrows arch but she didn't talk back, that was a good sign she was getting it. His authority was sinking into her thick head, he was the man and she was the woman.

"Also maybe some fresh strawberry shortcake for dessert. And pick yourself up some paperback romances or something, huh? I don't want Swami Shitstain's books in *my* house. Do I make myself clear?"

Ada chewed her lip but nodded, looking down at her bare feet. Eustace nodded in return, feeling satisfied that he'd talked slow and clear enough that she understood her role in this house. If she wasn't going to have a baby, then she was going to at least fulfill her duties as a wife - keep a neat household, cook, stay out of trouble, and be a supportive spouse, instead of getting caught up in all that other bullshit, like spending her time trying to understand things she could never possibly comprehend.

Ada would just have to accept she was only ever going to be a mediocre housewife and it was a waste of energy for her to pretend otherwise. The woman needed to grow up and face her reality, simple as that. Eustace was going to need a dependable partner if he was to ever truly fulfill his potential as a healer of the mind. He liked that phrase a lot, *healer of the mind.*

"Good, so go get dressed. I'll see you this evening."

"Have a good day, *honey.*" Ada might as well have spit the words on his loafer. The only thing that stopped her from screaming was the throbbing ribbon Eustace had left wrapped around her wrist.

When the front door closed Ada exhaled, *finally, he was gone.* She looked around the house, everything looked the same, but she could definitely sense a shift of some nature was taking place.

Her husband could deny Swami Nhincomhpoda all

he wanted, but Ada definitely saw her husband changing. Either he was connecting with a higher self… or he was having a breakdown. Either way it made Ada anxious. Why wasn't she reaching spiritual enlightenment and everyone else was?

The mantel clock she and Eustace had gotten for a wedding present rang in the sitting room. She figured she'd better start getting dressed and go to the market. It was going to take all day. An hour to do her hair, another forty minutes to figure out what to wear. Making sure she had all her buttons in place, plus a list of what she needed in her purse. And the thought of driving, all this spontaneity made her palms sweaty. Why was Eustace springing this on her? He knew how she liked to plan ahead.

As she pinned and sprayed her hair, Ada thought about the best route to the grocery store. They were doing construction on North Grand River avenue so she supposed she'd have to take Turner Street instead. She just prayed no other surprises came up, like tree cutters or garbage trucks taking up the road. Ada hated that, when she was stuck on a narrow road and forced to wait to pass a mail truck or service vehicle sitting right there in her lane. She sighed, feeling more overwhelmed by the moment. There was no way she was ever going to make it home by 2pm for her stories.

Coming downstairs, the phone rang in the kitchen. Ada really debated answering it. If it was her mother calling from California she'd talk all morning. And Ada always had trouble with salesmen. She'd insist she wasn't interested but still, they'd go on until she finally agreed to a visit or to donate money to the Fireman's charity or whatever it was they wanted. But… it might be Joann, who never had anything to do. Maybe she could go with Ada to the store! Then Ada wouldn't have to drive but just ride along and let Jo worry about the route and potential problems.

"Hello?" Ada rushed to pick-up just in case it was her friend.

"Ada?" Joann asked.

"Oh, Jo, I'm so glad it's you." Ada didn't realize how stressed she was from her morning and it had barely begun.

"Ada, sweetheart ,whatever is the matter?"

"Jo, it's just the worst thing. Stash snapped at me this morning and wants me to get rid of all my Swami Nhincomhpoda books. And he's combing his hair back and wearing his good slacks…. And now he wants me to go to the grocery store! Today! Can you imagine? As if I don't have enough to do and he just sprang everything on me this morning. Just demanding, demanding, *demanding*! Now I have to make an entire dinner plus find fresh strawberries! I'm just… I'm just…" Ada fell into tears. "He wants steak. I have to go to the market and there's construction." Ada felt herself struggling for air, trying to take in a breath.

"Sweetheart, get a paper bag. Just breathe. Do you have a bag?" Joann asked. Ada put the phone down and groped in the drawer for a lunch bag. The sound of the brown sack pulling in and expanding outward like a paper lung helped Ada regain a sense of composure. "Better?" She heard Joann's soothing voice a short time later.

"Yes. Thank you, Jo. You're an angel," Ada said, leaning against the counter, phone gripped white knuckle in one hand, the bag in the other.

"I have to run into town and get a few things, how about you ride along with me?" Joann offered.

Ada felt her shoulders sag, "I can never thank you, Jo. I'm so lucky to have such a good friend." The house-wife felt as if she wanted to sob all over again.

"It's no trouble. Go powder your nose and I'll be over a ten." Joann hung up.

Ada stood there a second, her hand shaking as she set the phone in its cradle. She looked at the break-fast dishes piled in the sink, obviously those would have to wait. She just couldn't deal with them right now. Also the stack of newspapers, she'd take care of them later. She didn't know when…but later. Maybe after her stories if she got home in time.

Ada caught a glimpse of her distorted reflection in the toaster, she really looked a mess. "Oh, fiddlesticks," she bemoaned her appearance. This day just got worse and worse.

+++

"Maybe Swami really did open up something in his mind? It is possible, and now he's just trying to deal with his loss of power. You know how men are, they don't like to feel as if they're out of control." Joann was saying while the two women pushed their carts around the supermarket. Their heels tapped, skirts swayed, they debated the merits of butter over margarine.

"Yes, I suppose that's true." Ada said, feeling calmer now. She held up a plastic yellow tub with red flowers, examining it. "Half the fat or fat free?" Ada asked, confused if it really made a difference. Did vegetables have fat to begin with? How do you take away half the fat? She really couldn't say. No one ever mentioned these things when she was a girl. Now there were more and more choices every year. Their basic groceries store had expanded to what felt like the size of a football field. Who needed 20 different kinds of cereal?

"I find margarine too thin. Burt likes his rolls richer. I'd go with butter." Joann said.

"Right. You're always right." Ada shook her head, how silly she was. Of course regular full-fat old fashioned butter tasted the best. The ladies continued to the baking aisle for the Spiffy mix. "So you just add water, an egg and butter? It seems much more complicated than that," Ada sighed. Why couldn't Stash just be happy with the buns that came in the bag over on aisle 3?

Joann chuckled, "It's not a science experiment. If I

can do it, anyone can. And hint: replace the water with buttermilk. It'll make it richer." She nodded her head, a twinkle in her eye as if she'd just dispelled a great family secret.

Ada dropped two boxes into her cart, nodding her head. "Okay dear, if you say so." The two women continued on. There wasn't really anything else they needed but neither felt like going home to clean, and their stories wouldn't be on for two hours. "So you really think Stash is just having some sort of spiritual reaction to Swami's session? Because he doesn't seem… enlightened, or connected to his higher self. If anything he seems… disconnected." Ada shook her head thinking about her husband this morning, how oddly slick and smug he looked.

Joann stopped by the ice cream freezer, murmuring about how everyone experiences spiritual growth differently. "Some people weep, some go crazy, others get angry, some except there is something bigger than themselves out there. Does that make sense? Take Burt for instance, we went home last night and oh my, I'm embarrassed to even say…..Ada?" Joann turned away from the chilled cartons of Rocky Road and Neapolitan when her friend failed to react to the potentially saucy story about her and Burt's spontaneous romp in the rec room.

Ada was wandering slowly down the center aisle as if entranced. "What?" Joann closed the door, looking after her friend.

"Huh? Nothing, I just thought…" Ada went further, squinting at the reflection of a shopper in the glass fridge doors that lined the back wall. It was as if someone were standing off to the side trying to decide what milk to buy. "Is that...?" Ada began to walk quicker. What was her husband doing at the supermarket now? It was past eleven, he was supposed to be in class till one. The figure walked off as she turned the corner.

"What?" Joann looked at the rows of milk, following her friend's gaze, trying to see what she saw. "Is it that busybody Jeanie, again? That woman-"

"No," Ada said, peering around. "I thought I saw Stash. How weird...I was almost sure it was him." Ada felt as if she were losing her mind again. The black slacks, white shirt and dark blazer. He was wearing those round glasses. Even though the figure looked distorted in the door she was sure it was him. When you live with a man decade after decade. You can just sense his presence, whether he's home or nearby or completely absent. What did Swami Nhincomhpoda talk about? Vibrations? Feeling other people's vibrations? Well, Ada thought for sure she could sense Eustace's vibes and he was shopping for milk.

"Stash? Why would he be here?" Joann was worried about her friend. She was a fragile little thing. Imagine not having a baby by forty and being married to a psychology professor. *What a nightmare*, she thought.

"I don't know. Silly, I suppose." Ada leaned against her shopping cart, so sure she saw her husband standing there.

The two women continued on. "Look, I'm going to

an art class this weekend. It's taught by this amazing spiritual artist, Raj Ado. I really think you should come. It'll be great fun and Raj is just a dream. Have you heard of him? I just think it could really help you get in touch with your creative energy. You know, feel the flow of the universe. Stash can't possibly protest that, can he?"

Ada laughed, "I suppose not. Yeah, maybe art is what I need."

+++

Ada stood in the doorway of the living room watching *The Guiding Light,* holding back tears that threatened to fall. "No, it can't be," she gasped. Sassy Bert was just diagnosed with uterine cancer. Ada placed a hand on her abdomen. What if she couldn't conceive a child because she had uterine cancer? She didn't think the doctors ever checked for that. Maybe she'd bring it up to Stash and see what he thought. He was sorta a doctor, she guessed. What did it matter? Ada knew these days she could be on fire and Stash probably wouldn't blink.

Once a woman was declared infertile she was as good as dead to her husband. She wouldn't be surprised if Stash was out there impregnating his students. *Where did that come from?* Ada shook her head, *how odd.* She'd never felt worried about Stash straying before. After all, he stayed by her side through everything. Why would he be unfaithful now? She knew him better than she knew herself, and if he was having an affair with anyone it was Dr. Freud. Ada chuckled to herself, *stupid Freud.* She'd spent almost her entire adult life hearing about that man.

There were times when she was dusting in Eustace's office and saw the framed photo of him sitting on the side table, the carved bust on his desk. *According to Freud…* "Fuck your theories, doctor!" she wanted to scream whenever Eustace brought him up as the voice of reason during a disagreement. As if by paraphrasing Freud somehow made him superior. Ada had been an art history major before she married Eustace, and still felt she knew more about the female brain than Eustace or his beloved Freud.

Ada didn't like to think about all she could have accomplished if she hadn't been swept up in the idea of getting married to a professor and having a family. If she'd know her uterus was defective maybe she would have stayed in school and become a spinster like Aunt Carol (who everyone suspected was a lesbian but were too polite to inquire further.) All her life Ada was horrified by the idea of being like Aunt Carol - single *and* a lesbian. But now? The idea of living alone or with another woman, maybe a woman like Joann, thrilled her on a level she never knew before. Imagine having a girlfriend to watch soaps with, paint nails with, to help put each other's hair in curlers before bed. And then, bed…*oh how naughty.* Ada thought of the idea of her and Joann…

The phone rang knocking Ada back to the reality of her marriage, Bert's uterine cancer, and her burning dinner. "Great balls of fire," she cursed herself and her daydreaming. Maybe she shouldn't have had that second cocktail. "Hello, Gish residence." She picked up the phone, tucking it between her shoulder and jaw, while trying to pull the tin of burning biscuits from the oven. "Hello?" she asked again but received only silence. She waited another second, listening, "Anyone on the line? I can't hear you. The connection is bad. Please call back." She hung up the receiver and kicked the oven door shut.

"Damn it all." Ada stood looking at her tin of half blackened biscuits. Maybe she could scrape the burnt part off the top, the insides might still be okay. How could she screw up something as straightforward as Spiffy Extra-Fluffy Dinner Roll Mix? It even said on the box *Easy As Pie*… "What a load of shit," Ada mumbled, thinking about what a pain the ass it was to make a lemon meringue pie.

She leaned against the counter, she was just not cut out for this housewife gig. She was an excellent student, but being a wife had turned her into a neurotic mess. Maybe she would take that art class with Joann. She remembered drawing and painting as an excellent way to calm her mind when things felt tangled up and overwhelming.

Ada jumped when she heard the front door slam. Eustace's keys and wallet dropped into the bowl on the side table. The coat closet door opened, a moment later it shut. Ada stayed in the kitchen waiting for her husband to come in and groan about his burnt biscuits. She stood there poised against the counter, thinking maybe if she looked cute he wouldn't yell at her.

"Stash?" she asked after a moment, waiting for him to come down the hall. The only noise was from the murmur of the television set in the other room. "Stash? I'm not sure about these dinner rolls." She tried to laugh it off. Maybe he'd think it was funny.

Still no reply.

"Eustace?" Ada leaned out into the hallway and looked towards the mudroom. The front door was closed and she noticed, oddly still locked. She often kept the door bolted during the day because of her fear of Jehovah witnesses. Whenever she saw them coming up the walk she hid behind the sofa waiting for them to go away. One time she was sure she saw them jiggle the handle. After that she couldn't stop thinking about possibilities of them bursting in and finding her cowering behind the sofa.

"Jesus Christ, just keep the door locked then, Ada," Eustace said when she told him about her fear for the seventh time. He never took her seriously. If she told him a tornado was heading directly for the house he'd probably tell her to calm down, and then go to bed as the place fell down around them. Then he'd blame it on her, like always.

Ada walked into the mudroom and looked at the small table with the disfigured blue catch-all plate she'd made last year in pottery class. It was empty. She opened the coat closet, the hanger was bare. Ada carefully closed the door and leaned against it, cradling her head, trying really hard to think. She was so sure she'd heard the door close, the keys clinking into the dish. Hell, she'd even heard the hard soles of Stash's shoes on the wood floor. The idea that she was going crazy again made her feel sick. No, that wasn't happening, she *knew* what she heard.

The lock turned and the front door flew open. Ada jumped out of her skin, her eyes wide as her husband walked in. "Ada? Good god, what's gotten into you? What are you doing?" Eustace looked her up and down, scrutinizing her.

Yes, she was dressed.

Yes, she'd removed her curlers.

Yes, she appeared to be a little tipsy.

"Stash," Ada finally managed to gasp. "I, uh, did you just get home?" He stood there a second, motioning for her to move away from the coat closet. "Oh, sorry." She kept looking at him.

"Ada, what's gotten into you? Of course I just got home. What do you think is on the other side of the front door? Another room? That maybe I was just hanging around on the porch?" He shook his head, *silly woman. One too many white Russians after lunch, again…*

Ada tried to laugh it off, rubbing her forehead, "Ha-ha, no, of course. But where um… Did you, uh, did you stop at the grocery store this morning?" she finally managed to get out.

"Why the hell would I do that? Ada, I said that *you* were supposed to go to the market. What do you do all day? Some of us actually work. I don't have time to teach and go grocery shopping. What's next? Do you expect me to come home and clean as well?"

"No, no, dear, of course not. It's just that I was there today with Joann and I thought I saw you is all." She turned to go back towards the kitchen, Eustace following.

"Huh, that's funny." Eustace walked across the hall to the living room, stopping at the bar cart.

"Is it?" Ada asked. She paused in the doorway, listening.

"Burt said something similar. He said he saw me at the diner, that I walked right past him but didn't turn around."

"Oh?"

"But I skipped lunch today to help a student. The poor thing was completely lost. I don't know how she ever ended up in my class." Eustace thought about the scattered brained twenty-one year old still going to school despite being married. Really? What were these feminists trying to prove?

"Help a student with what?" Ada thought back to the idea that her husband was sleeping with young, fertile students with flat tummies and long legs.

Eustace took a drink and sat down in his leather recliner near the window. He made a mental note that Ada

had failed to pick up the discarded newspapers and magazines that filled the side table. "Nothing really. It was ridiculous and a waste of everyone's time." Eustace said, thinking about the girl. She didn't have an original thought in her
head, but her ass had looked good in those red slacks of
hers. He thought about running a finger, perhaps a tongue
down the center of her legs. He bet she tasted like a lush
strawberry…

 "Dinner is almost ready," Ada rushed, turning away
to go back into the kitchen.

 "What?" Eustace shook the image of Annaleece
and her fitted trousers from his mind. "Wonderful," he followed up. He turned his eyes to the window, looking out at
the lake and its gentle ripples. Maybe he'd take the boat
out tomorrow for some fishing if the weather was nice. The
thought of spending a Sunday inside with Ada made his
stomach turn. "Do you have your book club with Joann tomorrow?" he asked. Maybe he'd get lucky and have the
entire day alone to fish and perhaps even try to work on his
manuscript.

+++

 "Well, Ada, you've really outdone yourself this
time." Eustace said looking at his dinner, of which he only
managed to eat one quarter of. It wasn't for lack of trying,

but the meat was tough as if he were chewing on a rubber tube. The biscuits, while being blackened on the outside, were somehow still raw on the inside. The green beans she'd chosen as a side were obviously from a can. There wasn't a potato in sight. The entire dish was swimming in melted butter with large flakes of red pepper.

"I've got pudding for dessert. I hope that's okay. The grocer won't have fresh strawberries for a few weeks." Ada said, glad Eustace was enjoying the meal she'd slaved over for five hours.

Her husband eyed her incredulously. "When did you get the time to make pudding?" He thought back to the last time Ada tried to make a custard. It was an all day event that included two boxes of tissues, a burnt oven mitt, several ruined cooking spoons, and ended with her hyperventilating in the bathroom. In the end they had to throw the saucepan out because the custard had coated the inside like horse glue. There went that Christmas. Ada hadn't attempted a pudding or custard since.

"I bought a box of the Spiffy Miracle Pudding Mix. You know, the instant kind. I just added milk and put it in the ice box!" Eustace looked at the gleam of satisfaction in Ada's eyes . He figured that the bowl of milk with chunks of brown powder in the fridge must be Ada's pudding. She probably had forgotten to whisk it. Looks like even a miracle couldn't save Ada's cooking.

"Very nice, dear," Eustace said, pushing his food around, trying to make it look like he had eaten more than he had. He should have known better than to insist Ada make an actual dinner. He would have been better off with one of those disturbing frozen meals of Salisbury steak and applesauce. They may have the texture of compacted sawdust but at least they were edible.

As Ada cleared the dishes, Eustace stood up to excuse himself before Ada got a chance to bring out the dessert. His stomach couldn't take much more. It had been in knots all day, as if he were on the verge of purging. He figured the sickness was a result of his migraine, which he wrote off to the shifting seasons, air pressure, etc. It would pass in a day or so. Eustace had hoped a decent home cooked meal would help, but he should have known better.

"Hey, do you want to eat our pudding in the den? That sounds fun right?"

"Not tonight Ada, dear." Eustace said, unbuttoning the top of his pants. The relief was immediate. The pressure from his waistband on his bloated abdomen had been a constant all day.

"But what about *Ozzie and Harriet*? Don't you want to see what happened after last week?" she asked, wiping her hands on her apron. "Come on, Stash. I'll pour you a whiskey. It'll taste marvelous with the chocolate pudding." Eustace thought the smile on her face might lead to a crack. He saw her lower jaw splintering and crashing to the floor, breaking into a thousand little shiny pieces the color of her coral lipstick. "Stash?" she asked when he failed to answer her. "Are you feeling alright?"

"Of course. Why would anything be wrong?" Eustace couldn't believe she was asking if *he* felt alright. She should look at herself.

"Just after yesterday, with Swami Na-"

"Don't say his name." Eustace said, biting the words. He wanted to rip that smug swami cult leader apart. The doctor's eye began to pulsate in its socket. It felt as if a blood vessel might rupture. The pressure would squeeze his eye out and it would land on the floor next to Ada's shattered jaw.

"Stash, you're being unreasonable. If you've had some sort of spiritual awakening it's only natural that-"

"Enough, Ada!" He cut her off again. Ada's mouth snapped shut and her expression grew cloudy, her eyebrows dipping to the center point of her brow. Eustace walked around the table towards her, Ada backed up, knocking into the sink. "Did you get rid of those books?" he asked her. It was quick, but he saw her eyes dart towards the doorway. Eustace nodded his head as if he understood. "Uh-huh, I thought I was very clear, Ada. I don't want that trash in my house." His voice was eerily calm.

Both stood there a second, but Eustace was the first to make a move, turning sharply and heading for the bedroom. Ada snapped out of it when she heard Eustace's pounding feet on the steps. "Stash!" she screamed, running after him. She couldn't believe he was acting like this. "Stash!" she yelled again coming to a stop in the bedroom doorway. "Don't," she said.

"I said to pick up some romance novels!" Eustace began ripping pages out of *A Familiar Face.* "Connect with your higher self! Visualization and manifestation! It's all hippie garbage!!" Eustace felt out of control, boiling over with a rage that had no reason. "All it does is cause trouble! Do you want to go back to the hospital, Ada?!"

Ada couldn't believe what she was seeing. Her husband was crimson. His skin slick with sweat as he tore out page after page from her book. She would have expected this type of thing from a communist, and while Stash had always had somewhat questionable political leanings he would never be mistaken for a communist.

"Stop! Stop it right now!" Ada ordered, rushing over. She attempted to pull the book from his hands but he threw it at her first.

"He just wants to help people!" Ada shouted, blocking her face before trying to save one of the other books, *The Serpent and the Woman.*

Eustace thought he was going mad. "Help people?!? You're completely naive if you believe that, Ada!" He said, trying to twist the book from Ada's hands.

Ada wrestled it free before jumping on the bed and off the other side. Eustace stood, hands balled in fists. "Give me that book, Ada. Swami Asswipe has never helped anyone!"

"Oh, like you?! You'll never help anyone! You're the hack! You've been writing that book of yours for how long now? Six years? Ha! You're the joke, Stash!" Ada jabbed her finger at him, laughing as loud as she possibly could. She could see her husband boiling over on the other side of the bed. She knew it was a harsh thing to say, but now she felt out of control. She was so sick of her husband always berating her for trying new things, but he never did anything! All he did was put down her interests and ambitions while insisting *he* was doing something important by "writing" some kind of self-help book, or developing his own "theory" like his precious Freud. But she'd seen him sit for hours just staring out the window at the lake!

Eustace took the last book from the bedside table, *Surrender and Live Beautifully.* "Do you seriously think this title even makes sense!? It's meant to appeal to simpletons! It's all just trash!" Eustace began pulling it apart, feeling really good when he managed to rip the top of the spine. He dropped the book's remains at his feet. When he was done he was huffing and puffing.

Ada was pressed against the far wall, horrified and ready to make a run for it if he tried to take the book she clutched to her chest. It was hard to say who the mad one was. By the end of it Eustace was bent over, leaning on his knees for support. He rolled his eyes up to glare at her.

"Jesus, Stash, you really should have someone look at that eye," was all she could say. It was redder than a lobster with a large white lump near the corner.

"To hell with my eye!" He pointed a stern finger at his wife as if she were little more than a child. "No more meditating or bullshit. If you need to work through your issues we'll get you an appointment with Dr. Saddler again. He's one of the best psychoanalysts in the country."

Ada rolled her eyes, "Fuck Dr. Saddler!" She'd had it with Stash thinking she was insane. She threw a book at him, nailing her husband square in the face, smashing his glasses into the bridge of his nose.

"Damn it, Ada!"

Ada laughed again as she dodged around him just out of reach. She ran out of the room. "Get your own damn pudding! I'm taking a bath," she sang. Eustace heard the guest bathroom door slam a second later.

The doctor stood in the now heavy quiet of the bedroom, only hearing the dull roar of water crashing into the iron tub one door over. *Just go in there and hold her under the water…* Eustace heard. It was tempting, very tempting, Eustace thought, scratching his chin. He looked at the ripped pages lying around like autumn leaves. Instead he picked everything up and decided to burn it.

On his way downstairs he paused outside the bathroom, thinking for a second how nice it would be to cram these pages down Ada's throat and hold her beneath the water. The paper would soak up the moisture, packing her mouth and clogging her airways. She could choke on that charlatan's advice.

Then she wouldn't be around holding you back anymore. She's the problem isn't she? That's why you can't focus because you have to constantly care for her. Wouldn't it be nicer if you just…

Eustace looked back toward the mirror at the end of the hallway, the reflection he cast showed him standing outside the bathroom door, except… it wasn't quite the same.

Eustace looked down at his arms full of ripped books, then back at the reflection. He jumped to see his mirror self cradling Ada's body, soaked and limp as a dishrag. Eustace swallowed, a page fluttered to the ground. Distracted, he looked away for a second at the paper scrap on the carpeting, then quickly back at the mirror.

He observed Ada's unsupported head sitting at an awkward angle, strained, slowly beginning to pull away. Her flesh bubbling and stretching before tearing off completely and hitting on the floor, leaving behind a ragged stump of a neck in which a wad of papers were stuffed like an overflowing trash bin.

"What are you doing out there? I can see your shadow under the door, Stash!" Ada yelled.

Eustace looked at the bathroom door, then turned towards the oval mirror, no, he was holding the torn remains of books. He needed to get his damn eyes checked and get some sleep. "Nothing, Ada, darling. Just cleaning up, so sorry," he said, walking on.

"Uh-huh," Ada snuffed, glad she'd hidden that vodka in the toilet tank because she needed it. All these years everyone said she was the crazy one, but maybe it was Stash all along.

Eustace stood in the backyard looking up at the soft light that filtered through the gauzy curtain in the upstairs window. *Ada,* he thought, wondering what he was going to do with her. The idea earlier was a revelation of sorts. He wondered if she was holding him back. He spent so much time worrying about her, picking up and doing her half of the chores that it was impossible for him to even think most of the time. She was a lousy life partner. Completely incapable of anything except causing a menace.

In the burn barrel, Eustace had tossed the pages and dowsed them with gas. The flames were a violent orange claws scratching at the otherwise flat twilight of the evening. "Honey, look. Is Stash and Ada having a bonfire? Wanna walk down and join them? We could take some margarita mix over." Joann was watching the dancing flame from their back patio. It was easy to see along the open yards all the way down the lake.

"Maybe not tonight, Jo." Burt walked out and stood beside his wife. He wasn't in the mood. Joann noticed his troubled expression.

"What is it?" she asked.

"Huh? Oh, nothing… Just, Eustace was acting a bit strangely today. I think the poor bastard really needs a break." Burt thought about that afternoon at the diner where he called out to his friend, who turned and looked at him but then kept walking as if he wasn't even there. Later when he confronted him, Eustace acted like he didn't know what the hell he was talking about.

"Ada was a little off too. In the market she thought she kept seeing Stash around every corner. I think they both need a long vacation."

"Or a good fuck," Burt laughed.

Joann elbowed him. "You're so filthy." The couple turned away from the flicker of the barrel six doors down. Burt took one last look before sliding the patio door closed. He shook his head, glad it wasn't him. Imagine being in your mid forties with a barren unsupportive wife and an unwritten book you've been claiming to be working on for years. And if he were being perfectly honest with himself, his friend wasn't looking so good these days. It was only a matter of time before Eustace had a heart attack, Burt thought.

"What are you thinking?" Joann asked, turning down the kitchen lights.

Burt looked at her, "Just that I'm glad it's not me," he said in reference to Eustace and Ada.

"Ha! I know!" The couple laughed.

+++

Ada got out of the bath and came into the bedroom,

the house was dark. It was by accident she noticed the ghost dance of the smoke outside. She looked out to see her husband standing near the burn barrel. *My books,* Ada thought, irritated her husband and had gone so far as to burn them. God, he was becoming more and more like her father every year! No wonder her mother drank so much.

Ada recalled about the vodka she kept hidden in the toilet tank, *thank god for the Russians,* she thought, then immediately chided herself for being so unpatriotic. She'd be thrown off all of her fundraising committees, lose her friends, and probably become an interest to the FBI if anyone thought she sympathized with those red commies. "I must just be tired," Ada murmured, continuing to look out at her husband as he stared into the fire.

"Ada, what are you doing?" She turned abruptly to see Eustace standing in the doorway, the smell of wood-smoke invading the room.

"But…?" She whipped around and looked out the window. "You were…" she trailed off, desperately search-ing the backyard for her husband who was just *RIGHT THERE.*

"That's right, I burned them. I don't want to hear an-other word about it, understand? Not one word."

Ada couldn't get a word out if she tried. All she could do was wonder if she truly was losing her damn mind. How much vodka did she drink? She'd never been drunk enough to hallucinate before. Stumble and pass out sure. Whip off her bra and sing while dancing on top of tables (she gave herself a pass on that one. It was New Years after all.) But this…

First she was certain that she'd seen Eustace in the supermarket. Then thought he'd come home, when he hadn't. Now he was just out in the yard and a second later in their bedroom. She couldn't help but walk over and touch her husband with a cautious hand.

"Whatever are you up to now?" Eustace asked her.

"I um, nothing. Maybe you're right. Perhaps Swami Nhincomhpoda *did* do something to my brain because…" she shook her head. "It doesn't matter now, does it? Good night," she said without much feeling. Ada slipped off her robe and got into bed.

Eustace stared at her for a second before walking into the adjoining bathroom. He thought if he could develop some strategies to help her, he could help anyone. So far he was feeling optimistic about it. It was as if the dirt had been wiped away from his mind's eye and he could finally see clearly.

The smoke from the fire had irritated his eye further, making it look a garish ruby. Eustace set his glasses near the bathroom sink, his vision immediately going fuzzy. He leaned forward so his nose was practically touching the glass.

He covered his irritated eye and his vision seemed fine, but in a boring way. Placing his palm over his right eye and looking through his left, his vision clouded up again and yet… somehow seemed pointed as if he had tunnel vision. The lights scattered and the sides became out of focus, but down there, down that black narrow cone he saw a flicker lingering. He wanted to reach out past the mundane and touch it.

The doctor was more than this. He was that spark fluttering just out of reach like a nervous bird tacked to a wall, its wings still fighting to carry it away. Eustace was going to grab that thing, be it fame or success or glory and make it his.

"Ouch! Damn it!" He recoiled when his face bashed into the mirror. He straightened up and much to his dismay that hole he wished to fall down had vanished, and he was simply in his bathroom. *This disgusting bathroom.* He had wanted to gut this bathroom ever since they moved in. Its hideous pink tiles, pink toilet, and sink made him feel as if he were stuck inside a chewed-up piece of bubble gum.

He picked at a line of stained grout on the wall. It wouldn't take much to demolish this place. Who ever heard of a pink bathroom? What did that make him? A girl's play-thing? Was this a dream house? Eustace looked around, no it most certainly was not. No wonder he couldn't get shit done, look at this place! What an embarrassing dump! How did he, Dr. Eustace Milhouse Walter Gish, ever find himself in such a place? He was of the old school leath-er sofas and dark walls, not kitschy pink foo-foo bullshit! It was ruining his focus. He just couldn't think surrounded by all this ridiculousness!

Ignoring his sleeping wife, Eustace walked swiftly through the bedroom, down the hallway, took the stairs two at a time. He went out the kitchen door, heading for the tool shed that sat down near the dock. *Perfect,* he thought when he'd located a twenty pound sledge hammer. *This'll knock that nonsense right out of there.*

He recalled when he'd bought this baby asking the clerk if they didn't have anything heavier, "what about fifty pounds?"

The clerk had actually laughed at him. "Even twenty might be too much for you, sir. You might want to think about a three pounder." It made Eustace's blood boil just thinking about the smirk on that guy's face. It had been nearly five years but every time Eustace went into that store and saw that guy he wanted to knock his teeth through the back of his skull. But right now Eustace had something better to do, turn those tiles to dust. Then he'd put in the sensible, mature white tiles that should have been in there all along. Perhaps he could actually take a relaxing bath, enjoy a leisurely shave without feeling like a complete puff.

The first smash right under the towel rack felt the best. Eustace nailed it creating a thunderous crack before several tiles splintered and fell away. Seeing that small bit of destruction felt good, really good. Eustace continued to swing the hammer, chipping the edge of the toilet tank, causing it to dribble water onto the floor. Fuck it! Eustace would replace the floor too! No worries.

"Stash! What are you doing?!" Ada stood terrified

in the doorway, clutching at her bathrobe, her eyes darting around unsure what to look at first. The demolished walls, the leaking toilet, or her mad husband in his good slacks and wrinkled sweaty white shirt. His eye with the bulbous sty that looked as if it might be infected.

Eustace rested the sledgehammer at his feet then wiped the sweat from his face. It felt good to feel so alive. He hadn't realized how scared and timid he'd been, as if he were hiding inside himself. "For once you were right, Ada. How can I ever help you or anyone if I can't truly know myself? This is me! I'm not going to continue living with this goddamn doll bathroom! I'm remodeling," Eustace said.

"At midnight? You decided to remodel the bathroom now?!"

"Sure, why not? It's not as if I can sleep thanks to the magic trick your little Swami Motherfucker did. Now every time I go to sleep I wake up feeling worse! I just need to think. My subconscious is telling me to embrace my deepest self, so what choice do I have? It's so clear, Ada," Eustace rushed towards her, grabbing her shoulders. Ada stood stiff in his arms. She couldn't take her eyes off the sledgehammer nearby.

"I think you should come to bed, Stash." she said, slow and cautious as she moved backward out of his reach. Her husband wasn't making any sense. What did a person's subconscious have to do with home demolition?

"What? *Now?* I'm just getting started. Don't worry, tomorrow is Sunday. I'll have the whole thing finished by tomorrow evening."

Ada knew there was no stopping him. For whatever reason her husband had decided now was the time to gut the bathroom. Either he was having an episode or she was. It was tough to say at this point. "I guess I'll just go to bed then…" her words were lost to the sound of smashing porcelain.

Eustace didn't bother to respond. He was feeling great grinding those annoying little pink tiles to dust. By tomorrow he'd have a whole new bathroom and then he could finally concentrate.

3.

"It's a painting class, Stash. I told you about it on Wednesday but you were just too busy with that stupid bathroom to notice." Ada said over dry toast and coffee.

"Do what you want, Ada. I don't have time to police you. I actually have things to do." Eustace said, thinking he had the perfect outline for his book. The steps were unfolding in his mind while he worked on the bathroom (that had stretched past Sunday to midweek.) Of course he would have gotten the job sooner done but the damn hardware store was closed on Sunday.

When he finally did get there Monday afternoon they didn't have the tiles he wanted. Then he was told he couldn't order them because the owner handled the buying and he was out of town the rest of the week.

Eustace had his day all planned out. So he supposed it was best that Ada would be out of the way and off at her painting class. It's not like she invited him to go. Maybe she'd finally learned her lesson.

"Burt's going," Ada said standing up, a little hurt that Eustace was acting so distant. All he cared about was his work and that stupid bathroom which was currently unusable. Thank god they had the guest bathroom down the hall otherwise they'd be in a terrible way right about now.

Her husband knew nothing about household repair

or construction, so she had no idea where this inspiration to get his hands dirty came from. She had married a gentleman who hired contractors, not this brute who insisted on smashing up a perfectly lovely little bathroom.

She'd cried on the phone to her mother after Eustace left on Monday for work. But her mother was less than helpful, and spent the whole time telling Ada about her sister Minnie's wonderful trip to Catalina.

"Thanks a lot, *mother*. But I really couldn't give two damns about Minnie or her stupid family. You know how much I can't stand that weasel Chip! And their children are just horrible brats!"

"Ada!" her mother said, astonished.

"We'll talk soon." Ada slammed down the phone and lit a cigarette. *Fuck Minnie and her stupid Catalina vacation.* Ada hoped her sister got sunburned. And Chip was no prize. He'd pinched Ada's ass last year at Christmas. Thank goodness Eustace wasn't a pig. He'd never touch a woman's ass, he didn't even touch her ass.

At least, Ada hoped she was right. She figured either her husband was connecting with his higher self, having an affair, or a midlife crisis. Whatever the reason, she could only hope all this nonsense would soon pass.

+++

Eustace looked around at the unfinished bathroom. The water was turned off. The sink (which turned out to be iron and not porcelain) was still bolted firmly to the wall. The remnants of the toilet were tossed out the window. There was a grimy black hole in the floor where the sewage pipe now sat exposed. Eustace stood gazing at it. That was all he did the previous evening, for hours…

After he woke last night he went into the bathroom and sat on the edge of the tub (which was white so he decided it could stay.) He leaned forward and stared at that hole. The doctor was sure he heard whispering from somewhere down the drain, telling him exactly what he needed to write, to do, to fulfill his life's purpose. It was as if the drain were a direct line to his higher self.

His wife banged on the door constantly demanding to know just what was he doing in there? If the place was cleared out and he didn't have any new tiles what could he *possibly* be doing in there?!

"I'm busy!" He'd yell, punching the wall, kicking debris, irritated she couldn't just leave him alone for two seconds so he could think. Ada was worse than a child. She was always watching him, picking at him. So it was a relief when Saturday rolled around and she reminded Stash that she was going to that frivolous painting class.

Eustace looked at his watch, it was only 8:30am, but maybe he'd get to the hardware store early. That way he could order the tile before the owner got busy. Then he could get home and write a few pages for his book. He bet

Ada and Joann would go out for cocktails and pie after the class. If that was the case, Ada wouldn't be home till at least three. He had plenty of time.

The hardware store wasn't far, a twenty-five minute walk. Eustace had taken to walking most places in the past week. He felt himself becoming more like his true self every day. While Eustace was sure that Swami Assface had done nothing directly to help with his new outlook, maybe in some roundabout way it allowed Eustace to get in touch with a part of his unconscious mind. The trauma of being drugged and put under group hypnosis had jolted something loose within himself.

Since that evening at the community center Eustace's dreams had been getting more and more intense. Often he found himself coming into the bathroom when sleep failed him. Sitting in the dark, staring into the unknown black laced with whispers, helped him sort through his knot of thoughts. Eustace found his ideas regarding his soon-to-be new book were slowly becoming clear. Staring at that mucky hole in the floor, it felt as if he were simply sitting with an old friend shooting the breeze.

Eustace just knew there was something inside of himself that was always there, a spark of greatness that would put him up there with Freud. He just needed to write down what the voice in the sewage drain said, get this bathroom retiled, and all would be well.

"Dr. Gish?" The voice was like a song. Eustace over up into the eyes of Annaleece. Her low cut blouse was filmy and her slacks tight so they outlined her underwear. *Disgusting,* Eustace thought.

Unimpressed, the doctor pulled out a cigarette and lit it casually before saying, "Oh, good morning Annaleece. What brings you here so early?"

She smiled, "I work here part-time," she said, gesturing to Merritt Hardware. "I thought you knew that."

"No, I didn't. I'm waiting for the owner to open the damn place up. I need some tile for my bathroom. Is he always so late? It's unprofessional." Eustace glared back at the shop.

But Annaleece only giggled, she loved grumpy old men, and Dr. Gish was such a catch. She'd taken one of his classes as a freshmen and didn't think much of it. But then for some reason she saw him last week and had this unrelenting urge to switch out of two other classes and into his abnormal psych class, plus his Freud and theory class. "I like your new glasses. They make you look so distinguished," she said, cocking her head to one side like a dim puppy.

"Yes, I know." Eustace was already tired of her insipid small talk. In fact he was tired of women all together.

She moved closer and Eustace felt heat rising to his face. "Doctor?" she whispered as if they were in cahoots with one another. He looked down his nose at her, exhaling smoke into her face. She didn't seem to mind and smiled through the haze.

"Yes, what is it, Annaleece?" Eustace wished that

the deadbeat owner would move his ass. He looked at his watch, it was 8:56 am. He couldn't show up to open four minutes early? Unfuckingbelievable. The world was going to hell in a hand basket.

"I want to see you again. I keep thinking about last time and-" she paused before leaning closer to whisper in his ear, "it makes my panties so wet."

"Excuse me?!" Eustace shoved the girl away.

"OH!" Annaleece stumbled back off her stocky platforms before tumbling into the gutter.

"I don't know what you're referring to but there will be no more of that. Don't you have any respect for yourself?" Dr. Gish looked down at the girl as she sat there stunned.

"But Eustace, Tuesday we…uh, you, well… you know what happened! You were there!" Annaleece climbed back to her feet and attempted to regain some composure. "You," she dropped her voice, "fucked me in your office and said you loved my tight cunt. *You* came on to *me*!"

Eustace couldn't believe what a sad delusion girl Annaleece was turning out to be. This was exactly why married women should be at home and not at university. Sure, Eustace pegged her as having a mild borderline personality disorder, but he didn't take her for a pathological liar as well. "I think you need to go home, Annaleece. Perhaps you should think about seeing the campus counselor. I could make a call if you'd like."

"What?" she asked, astonished. "I'm not the one

who's crazy here. You fucked *me*! You came on to *me*!"
She shouted with more force this time. Thankfully, there
was no one on the street so early on a Saturday morning
to hear. "Unbelievable," she looked around as if she had no
idea what was going on. The girl was clearly having a hys-
terical episode.

"Annaleece, do you hear yourself now? Perhaps
you should take some time off school. Such demanding ac-
ademics can be trying for the young female mind. There's
a reason women are the weaker sex. Please, let me call
your husband to come pick you up. That damn owner
should be here any moment, I could ask to use the phone
and-"

Annaleece was backing away. "What?" she muttered again, shaking her head as if this whole thing was
completely surreal. "I'm on a full academic scholarship.
Weaker mind? Fuck you, Doctor Gish!" She turned and ran
out into the road without looking.

"Annaleece!" Eustace watched the owner's red
Buick coming around the corner, slamming into the willowy
twenty year old, throwing her several feet across the black-
top. The sound of rubber on pavement, the dull *thunk!* of
flesh meeting steel, then skidding along the ground, was
enough to make Eustace's stomach turn.

"Annaleece?!" The owner, whom Eustace immediately recognized as the grinning asshole who sold him
the twenty pound sledgehammer, stumbled from his car
without even killing the engine. "What happened?" he

screamed standing over the bleeding blonde. "Why was she in the road? I didn't see her, I didn't see her!" he cried, falling to his knees.

Eustace looked from the girl to the man and back again. "She was going home because you were late. She didn't think you were coming. Perhaps if you're going to run a business you should learn to be on time." Eustace said before turning and walking back towards home.

More people were gathering now. He could hear the howling of the shop owner, begging forgiveness from God. The doctor couldn't help but grin a little, he finally got one up on that smug owner. Let's see him act so high and mighty next time Eustace went in there to buy some nails or a screwdriver. Little prick had it coming. And as for Annaleece, clearly she was having a breakdown. If she couldn't hack it at school he doubted she had much of a future anyway. She probably would have ended up a neurotic basket case like his Ada. It was better this way, he thought.

Though one thing did nag at him, the idea that he fucked her last Monday afternoon. This idea seemed impossible as he left promptly after his last class and went directly to the hardware store before heading home. He never even went by his office, so what kind of hallucinations was the woman having to imagine such a scenario? The same with Ada and her delusions of him shopping for milk. It disturbed him to say the least. So many troubled women, he really needed to get his shit together and help them.

(Note: Eustace dismissed Burt's strange claim of seeing him in the diner, because Burt was known to knock back a few drinks most afternoons. Eustace wrote the claim off to Burt being drunk and nothing more.)

+++

Eustace spent the rest of the day wandering between his dilapidated bathroom on the second floor and his office on the first floor, where he spent half the time trying to remember what the sewage drain told him and the other half trying to type it all out. The problem was the voice was so soft he couldn't always make out what it was saying. The words were all jumbled in his brain.

"Fuck," he said, raking his fingernails over his face, tearing them down his neck. He shoved away from his desk, knocking his chair over, and went back upstairs to stare at the black hole in the floor where the toilet once grew. If only he could just get whatever it was to come into focus, then it would all make sense! His thoughts from his higher self would become clear.

After the sewage hole, surrounded by broken tiles, failed to answer his follow-up questions, Eustace got up, feeling defeated and stared at himself in the mirror. He had red streaks down his face from his nails. His left eye looked wet, almost as if it had been punctured inside, with blood pooling just below the surface. He wanted to prick it, like when you dip toast in a soft egg. Just break the surface tension and let it flow out.

The pressure behind it was almost unbearable. The area where he'd picked open the angry sty with a sewing needle still looked raw with a lemon crystalline scab he had to pick off each morning in order to open his eyelid. Ada wanted him to go to the doctor, but Eustace assured her he was perfectly fine. She said it looked like the sty had turned into an ulcer and was surely infected.

Carefully, he set his glasses aside and switched on the vanity lights to get a better look. *Oh, yeah, right there,* he saw the little black dots speckled on the surface like flattened insects on a windshield. Maybe he could just squeeze it gently like a pimple. Perhaps he did have an infection and pus had built up back there. Eustace figured, what could it hurt? After all, he did (loosely speaking) go to medical school and was *technically* a doctor.

In the medicine cabinet Eustace looked over his options. Tweezers? no, that didn't seem right. He wasn't pulling out a sliver. Dental pick? *Stupid,* he thought, of course not. He wasn't some lunatic. There was Ada's sewing needle he had previously stuck in the sty. It was a little cruddy, but sharp and tiny nonetheless. He could stick it in just below the surface and see if that did anything. Hell, he would jam it all the way back if that's what it took.

At first he thought it was only Ada distracting him. Then he thought perhaps it was also the horrid pink bathroom. But maybe this was it, this eye had to be dealt with. Then he could finally get some sleep and actually focus on his work. He just didn't know where his head had been this past week and half. Something had to change.

Eustace swabbed the sewing needle with iodine. Leaning close to the mirror, using steady hands, he decided to prick the area just above the sty wound on his eyelid. Maybe the ulcer had invited infection in. Fuck if he knew, it could be all matter of things. A combination of irritants from that dirty hippie jamboree, seasonal allergies, sinus pressure, maybe he scraped it in his sleep. Well, he assured himself, it would feel better once he got it all flushed out.

He could only hope it would be as simple as that, before momentarily thinking *shit what if it's a tumor?* The fuzzy vision, pain, voices…*shut the fuck up, stop being a pansy ass,* he silently berated himself. It was just an infection. He was going to drain it, then afterward he would make a drink and go write. Simple as that. He wasn't Ada, everything didn't have to be so damn complicated.

Needle poised, Eustace inhaled when he felt the tip press against the tender edge of his inflamed sclera, then exhaled as he pushed it in. He focused on the sound of his breath, along with the immense satisfaction he felt when he removed his hand to see the narrow sliver of steel had remained in place, jutting from his eyeball. "Just like acupuncture." Eustace remembered when Ada used to run around trying to stick pins in his back insisting it would help with his qi.

But Eustace's satisfaction was short-lived when what looked like a red curtain fell over his reflection, casting his image in a bloody light before fading to black on one side.

"What the…?" He lunged at the mirror, smashing his fist through the glass, silver shards fell like broken stars around his feet. He was sure this was supposed to help, but now he couldn't see shit! His reflection looked more out of focus than ever! He had to remove the poison. Fumbling, Eustace located the sewing needle and yanked it out, letting it fall down the sink drain.

One large warped triangle of mirror remained in the frame, he attempted to focus through his annoyance and pain. Straining, he squeezed the damaged eyeball with the ends of his thumbs "Come on, you bastard," he growled at his eye. Maybe it was a parasite. He pictured a maggot curled up inside, along with jelly pus swirled in a cream paste.

"There, you go…" Eustace said, pushing the infection out. He thought he felt the thin film on his outer eye rip, "Ugh!" he spat, forcing himself to continue applying pressure despite the rapid burn he felt, as if the simmering match that was there before had turned into an entire flaming box.

Reality seemed to waver, and Eustace felt flies swarming in his ears. He had to sit or he was going to fall. His knees buckled, he had no choice but to slide down the wall, and sit among the fractured mirror pieces and smashed tiles. He took several deep breaths, his skin was clammy and yet he had sweated through his clothing. The dampness gave him the chills. "It's okay, you're going to be okay," he assured himself.

Eustace rubbed his fingers together, feeling the stickiness of drying blood. He held his hand close to his right eye, examining the gore. The feeling hit him, and Eustace couldn't help but laugh. He did it. It felt so good to have that poison out of his head. He wiped the hot trickle of fluid off his face and slung it down the sewage hole beside him like an offering. Now he just had to disinfect the wound.

Go to a doctor, pugh! Eustace thought when he dumped iodine into the pulpy socket, feeling it run over down over his cheek, staining his skin the hue of a rotten apricot. Eustace groped for a chunk of mirror and held it up, examining his work. *Damn,* he thought, maybe he shouldn't have waited so long. Now look at the mess he'd made. The sight though, no matter how raw, was comforting to say the least, like when a woman finds that perfect dress or you realize avocado green is *the perfect shade* for that new shag carpet. It just clicks into place and you immediately love the look of it.

Eustace slumped against the wall, pain giving way to a calm relief. Next time he wouldn't wait so long to correct minor annoyances should they grow into larger ones. He'd definitely learned his lesson.

The hallway was black but for a light that poured in through a set of exterior doors. There were mounds of stray sand littering the floor. For once Eustace wasn't heading for the mirror or that shadow he often saw twisting in the dark, but instead was turned away facing the set of exit doors. A whispering draft was coming through, blowing sand in his face.

The room door closest to him was cracked open, just a hair, barely noticeable. Imagine his surprise when he pushed it and saw yet another mirror inside. This was beginning to feel like a fun house. But the more he looked, the more it dawned on Eustace, that perhaps these weren't mirrors at all, but windows to another level of consciousness.

His figure moved in a blurred motion, as if he were being photographed with a delay, streaks stretching out behind him. He heard the breathy voice in his ear, *hello,* it said.

It was a comfort to the doctor who responded with the same tone, "Hello."

While this figure looked and acted like a better version of himself, somewhere in the back of his mind Eustace knew it wasn't really him. Maybe some facet of himself, but surely not truly a flesh and blood human by any means. The mirror self held up a hand in a subtle wave,

Eustace mimicked him. When Eustace touched his eye, the other did the same. They were surely linked by this dark tunnel that flowed from one to the other.

Visualize what you want, Eustace thought and the other came more into focus. Yes, it was indeed an aspect of the doctor.

"What are you trying to tell me?" Eustace's banging on the glass made the image before him tremble. He had to stop wasting time if he ever wanted to get his book done.

The figure smiled, looking as if a child had drawn a grin with a smear of charcoal, distorting it. Eustace exhaled, frustrated.

The doctor felt haunted, like this double had been following him his whole life, always kneeling behind him. Now Eustace saw him, but still the thing wouldn't fill in the blanks.

The doctor leaned his forehead to the glass, he was so tired. He wanted to fall through the mirror and never wake up. He was a failure, he would never be as great as his mind. The medium of physical reality was simply a barrier. How could he ever develop a working psychological theory if he didn't even know himself?

With his one good eye, Eustace watched the shadow mimic his motions, lying its face on the mirror's surface close to his, so Eustace could see directly down into that glistening black hole. A kaleidoscope of glassy colors turned in the darkness, reminding Eustace of morning sun breaking through beveled glass.

Soon cold gusts of wind picked-up, silently carrying the answers Eustace sought. The shadowy aspect of himself was now smeared with his physical person, a sticky tar patch packing itself into the empty socket of his head. *A magnet,* that's what Eustace thought. The Other was sticking to him like a magnet to steel, because they were the same.

Eustace chuckled as he wandered along the walls and ever expanding halls, *it was that easy.* All this time he was trying to hear the voice with his ears, see things with his eyes, but that was all wrong. What he really needed to do was shut off his senses to the outside world, and just listen to the voice on the wind knocking at his door.

The puzzle of words he'd been trying to decipher all week was clear now. The missing pieces were filled in and suddenly just like that step 1 was done.

Now Eustace needed to rid himself of his old thoughts. Whatever was keeping him from wellness had to go.

+++

Eustace was leaning against the wall among broken glass and debris, feeling the drying remains of his eye on his hands and face. The cloying odor of curdled blood telling him he was awake, it wasn't all simply a fantastical dream. He'd had a true break-through and all he wanted to do was show it to others.

He struggled to his feet and placed his hands on either side of what remained of the medicine cabinet door. The few shards of the bathroom mirror reflected this realization back to him. He looked straight ahead, his fear and anxiety bleeding from his head wound. Eustace saw the cosmos in that yawning wound where his eye once sat.

It was like connecting with a lost friend who helped remind you who you are and where you came from. His blind spot now reflected something greater than the material world, and he saw it all. "I've missed you, old friend," he said to his broken reflection.

The front door slammed, startling the doctor and forcing him to turn away from the battered cabinet. How long had he been in this bathroom? Ada was home already? She'd just left a few hours ago… and yet he heard her bustling around downstairs while he continued to stand there, bracing himself on the wall, seeing his entire book right there within himself where he always knew it was. Even if he never wrote anything down he had it right there where he could see it.

Eustace turned back to the mirror, his gore clodded face stained with iodine was a mess. Ada was going to freak out, like always. He turned away to locate a bandage, a towel, something to clean himself up with.

However, the smudge that passed as Eustace's reflection remained a few seconds longer, staring straight ahead, before dissolving like water boiling to steam.

4.

Ada set her canvas and paint set on the dining room table. She figured it was as good a place as any to work on her painting. The room had wide open windows that looked out over the lake at the bottom of the garden. The morning and afternoon sun would cast a perfect natural light most of the day. The art teacher, Raj, said that being close to nature with views of water was a great way to connect with the muse, and her dining room sounded like the ideal spot. Ada hoped so.

She looked around the room and felt uninspired by the mauve walls, the blue braided rug, the buttery yellow hutch that held gold-rimmed wedding dishes. The like-new table and chairs that should have been heavily worn after all this time dominated the space. She felt like she was in some showroom not her own house and certainly not a studio.

For a second she stood there staring out at the rolling surface of the lake. Turning back to the dining room she thought about how good it would feel to take her cobalt oil pastel out and run it along that pristine mauve wall. Her mother had chosen the color, but Ada never cared for it. She always wanted something vibrant and fun, orange maybe. Just any color but mauve or beige. Suddenly the blank canvases she brought home didn't feel very inspiring but those ugly walls did.

"Ada?" Eustace stood in the doorway, a hand towel stuck to his face with surgical tape. He had failed to find gauze and cotton squares. "What on earth do you think you're doing?" her husband asked.

Ada had shoved the large dining table against the far wall, leaving a noticeable heavy scrape on the wood floor. She was now in the process of moving the chairs and kicking the rug out of the way.

"Stash?!" She was equally shocked to see her husband with blood dried to his shirt and a towel bandaged to his head, his hair sticking up in all directions. He looked like he got into a fight with a bear.

"Just a little renovation wound, nothing to worry about. It looks worse than it is." Eustace reassured his wife. He was surprised when she shrugged and went back to assessing the long wall that separated the kitchen and the dining room.

Without pause Ada pulled down the paint-by-numbers portrait of a German Shepard her lesbian aunt had given to the couple as a Christmas present a few years back.

"I always hated that thing." Ada said, tossing it aside.

Eustace continued to watch his wife flutter around like a bird in a cage. "So Ada, what is all this?" he asked, gesturing to the ruined room.

"My new art studio," Ada said. "At least, maybe it

will be? Oh Stash, I don't know…I thought maybe if I painted a mural, added some color, it would help really liven
stuff up." But Ada looked at the long bare wall and felt stupid. "Maybe I should put it all back, but then where am I
going to paint?" She felt on the verge of tears. The day had
been so good. She loved connecting with the other ladies,
but now at home she felt unsure of herself and what she
truly wanted.

"Ada?" Eustace said, coming over and placing his
hands on his wife's shoulders. The pair faced the wall. "I
think I can help you," he said.

Ada sniffed, "What, with painting?"

"Not the painting itself, but maybe give you a boost
of confidence. That's all anyone ever really needs. He
turned her so she was facing him. "Close your eyes," he
told her. After a second Ada managed to tear her gaze
away from her husband's ruined face and close her eyes.

Eustace went on, "Now picture that inside of your
chest is a bird."

"A bird?"

Eustace flexed his hands, forcing himself to remain
calm and focused. "Yes, Ada, a bird. And in your brain are
worms."

"How horrifying."

"It is, isn't it?" Eustace looked at her a moment,
thinking about how nice it would be to crush her face in.
He cleared his throat. "I want you to focus on that bird and
let it out of your ribcage. Picture it flying upwards into your

head. Once there it will pick and peck and pull each and every one of those worries from your mind."

"Worries? I thought you said there were worms," Ada said.

"The worms are the worries. Worries and fears and doubts."

"Oh, okay," Ada said, her eyes still closed.

"Great. So let the bird loose and allow it to feed on all of the fear and anxiety that cripples you Ada."

Ada giggled.

"What is it?" Eustace asked, briefly annoyed that his wife was laughing at this great gift he was giving her.

"The feathers, I think I can feel them, Stash. Yeah, they…" her voice began to sound wispy and far away. "The bird… it's there." Ada lifted her hands and cradled her head. "I can feel it moving around and…ah!" Ada crumbled to her knees, Eustace held her firm, guiding her to the floor. "Stash, Stash it hurts."

She folded in on herself, lying still a second, trying to breathe through the discomfort. Ada had plenty of experience with head pain of all sorts, from PMS headaches to hung-over migraines but this was something else. Soft feathers with a razor blade beak pulling out at worms edged with barbs.

"Better?" Eustace asked after Ada laid still for a moment, scared to move lest if inflame her brain further. Finally she managed to lift her head and crack open her eyes.

"I… yes," she said, noticing the pain was rapidly subsiding. "Jesus, Stash. Is that part of your book?" she gasped, sitting up.

"Yes Ada. And it's only step 1. But don't worry it will get easier." Eustace assured her. "So how do you feel?"

Ada searched her mind, suddenly all she could see were bright colors, a floor to ceiling portrait and her husband. "I want to paint you," she said.

"Me?" The pair rose from the floor.

"I have too, Stash. Just um, here… just sit right here for a moment." Ada pulled a dining chair into the middle of the room and urged her husband to sit. Eustace humored the woman just glad to see his wellness practice was working.

Ada had a charcoal stick in her hand, rapidly she began to sketch lines across the wall. All the while talking about how she was going to do this and that and these colors and add this here, and on and on…

Eustace sat back, taking his cigarette case out of his pocket and lighting the end of a Lucky Strike. He was a fucking genius. Sure, he had to sacrifice his eye in order to truly see his path, but in the end it was all going to be worth it.

First he'd fix Ada, then when she was no longer an embarrassment he'd be ready to present his methods to the world. Husband and father would write to thank him. Women line up to get their books sighed. Oh yeah, Eustace saw it all.

"There! What do you think?" Ada asked, jumping off the chair. "Stash?" Ada looked from her sketch to her husband who had nodded off. "Stash!" she shook him awake.

"What? Oh it's, uh…" Stash squinted at the wall, remembering why he was sitting on this chair in the first place. "That's it, huh?" he said.

"Well, it's not done yet, obviously…" Ada trailed off, chewing her fingernails feeling nervous for a reason she couldn't quite understand.

"Obviously." Eustace said. Her drawing was nothing more than black scratched lines at sharp angles, barely resembling anything human let alone him. He tilted his head, he guessed he could see a figure of some sort.

"I don't get it. Is it supposed to be modern or something?" Eustace shook his head, he never really understood art like this. He liked the raw power of Jacques-Louis David or Caravaggio. The last time Ada dragged him to an exhibit Eustace wanted to puke. *What worthless trash,* he thought as Ada cooed at the massive canvas painted solid red, or the bent tangle of wire that represented a ballerina in motion.

"Look at that, it's so beautiful. Do you think I'm too old to take ballet lessons?" Ada asked at the time.

Eustace looked harder at the portrait sketch Ada had drawn on their dining room wall.

His wife came to stand beside him, "Well, it's um..." Ada struggled to explain her intentions behind the piece, "It's not done," she finally concluded.

"So you've said."

"You can't expect a masterpiece in one day, Stash. Gosh! Do you know that some painters only paint one inch a day! That's how much detail they use. What do you want me to do? Just slap some paint on the wall and call it a day? Fuck it, I'm taking a bath!" Ada ran from the room. Eustace heard the bathroom door slam minutes later.

"Ada?" He climbed the stairs and saw the door to the guest bathroom open. "Are you using…" he trailed off and walked through their bedroom and tried the door-knob, it was locked. "Ada? What are you doing in there?" He knocked at the door. "Ada, you lunatic, the water is shut off! Go take a bath in the guest room."

Silence.

A minute later Eustace heard running water through the door. *What the hell?* He pushed his ear against the wood to listen. Sure enough, it was the sound of the bath filling up, his wife was humming as if she didn't have a care in the world.

"Did you say something, Stash?" she finally called.

Eustace stood back, trying to determine if she was messing with him or not. "I said the water is shut off, dear. Why not use the guest bath?"

"Ha! It seems just fine to me. It almost feels like you want to keep this room to yourself. Now go away," she said, humming louder.

Eustace opened his mouth to argue, but held back, turning away in frustration. He'd had such a great day, now Ada was holed up in the bathroom like she owned it. So much for any further rumination on the mysteries of the universe or getting started on chapter 2 step 2 of his method (which was still in need of a catchy name). He'd have to go stare out the window like everyone else. However, he told himself, if Ada thought she owned that bathroom she had another thing coming.

5.

"If you ask me the idea is outdated anyway," Burt said. Eustace watched mustard from his colleague's sandwich dribble down the front of his shirt. He noticed despite Burt being overweight and middle aged he was always dressed nice, his shirts starched and his pants pressed. "What? What is it?" Burt followed Eustace's gaze. "Oh fuck, Jo's going to have my head, ha-ha." He laughed it off while trying to remove the yellow condiment with a napkin.

"You're just smearing it," Eustace told him.

"Good thing Jo knows her way around a washing machine, eh?"

Eustace didn't want to talk about the wives. "What the hell do you mean by outdated?" He turned their conversation back to his book idea. He was trying to explain to Burt how each step would be a chapter. Six chapters in total plus an introduction.

Eustace had a revelation last night after Ada finally got her ass out of the bathroom and he was able to get in there. He was disturbed to see the tub was dry and there wasn't any steam on the window. The broken pieces of mirror were still on the floor, yet Ada didn't say a thing about it. But, ignoring his psychotic wife, he turned to the large shard of mirror still dangling in the frame.

Removing his bandage, he was pleased to see the ooze and bleeding had stopped. Eustace liked the yawning gap. He thought if he looked closely enough he could see through to the other side, doors stretching out down the long corridor, the lights flickering to illuminate his path.

After deciding he liked his new look, the doctor turned and stared down into the sewage hole and woke up aching the next morning. "You slept on this floor all night?" Ada asked. If Eustace didn't know any better he thought she sounded a little jealous.

The most amazing idea for step number 2 had hit him during the night. It was so clear in his brain he didn't even have to write it down. It was there all along, just as he knew it was, locked away till he was ready.

Eustace gave Ada instructions for her to follow while he was at work. She was to take anything that remained within herself that caused anxiety, sadness, and worry, anything that crippled her, and she was to purge it.

"It would be a short and simple book," Eustace went on. "A step-by-step guide mostly aimed at the female market. You know how desperate they are. Haven't you heard of housewife syndrome? This market is dying for a clear and simple self-help book. I tried out the first two steps on Ada, and she seems to be responding well. This is it, Burt, I know it." Eustace took a gulp of his coffee. Burt was still looking at him. "Are you looking at my eye again, Burt? I told you I'm fine."

"Uh, sorry, right, yeah. You did see a doctor right? I just don't get how…"

"Burt! I asked you a question," Eustace said.

Burt cleared his throat, trying to ignore the unsettling feeling his friend was giving him. "I don't know buddy. I mean sure, a self-help book is great, but aren't there millions of them? I just think if you're so keen on this great idea, and it does sound promising, you should think about doing something a little more cutting edge. If modern women are so busy why would they take time to read your little nothing book instead of like Swami Nhi-"

Eustace cut him off, "What do you propose then, Burt? Should I include pictures? Are you saying your wife is so dumb she needs a picture book to help her?"

"Whoa, don't get defensive. That's not what I'm saying. I'm just thinking that apart from Saturday book club Jo doesn't have much time to read."

"Well, maybe if she spent less of her day watching that nonsense on the TV she'd have more time." Eustace took an aggressive bite of his toast and dropped the crust on the table.

"That's what I'm saying," Burt said, his voice going up a notch. "I always thought, what if the Swami or something like that had a TV program? Then all the little housewives could get together and spend thirty minutes getting in touch with their higher self or whatever they call it."

Eustace turned this idea over in his head. The more he thought about it the more he loved it. It would be better than a picture book. He could slowly and clearly explain to the women exactly what he was talking about. "Fuck Burt, you clever bastard!" Eustace sat back, almost smiling, feeling all the pieces were coming together and the universe was behind him.

"Plus the students need something for their final project and I can't find anything else for them to work on," Burt followed up, hoping Eustace wouldn't take offense. But the doctor barely heard him.

"Six episodes with one airing per week. I could walk them through each step…" he mused out loud.

"Sure, that sounds great. But uh…" Burt paused.

"What?" When Eustace looked directly at him, despite his face being bandaged, Burt felt unsettled.

"You might have to do something about-" he motioned to his face.

Eustace chuckled in a way Burt had never heard before, it was deep and unnatural for his friend. "Don't worry about a thing Burt. Just let me know when you need me." Eustace stood up.

"We still have fifteen minutes," Burt said, checking his watch. He didn't want to be stuck in his basement classroom any longer than he had to. Whenever he got there early all the overly ambitious students showed up and wanted to talk to him. He hated that.

"I've got things to do, Burt. A good idea doesn't just happen on its own. It takes years of work and self-reflection for it to finally manifest."

"My grandfather started the Spiffy Mix Company on a whim because he liked my grandma's rolls," Burt said.

"Uh-huh. I'm sure many men loved your grandmother's rolls, but that's baking mix, Burt. I'm changing lives here."

Eustace turned to leave but ran into the waitress. "Oh, so sorry." He looked at the expression of confusion on her face. "What is it Helen? It's a wound. It's not like I'm growing a second head." Eustace said to the waitress. Jesus, everyone was so shocked by his face bandage. He'd never be able to fully reveal himself to the public; they wouldn't be able to handle it. He'd have to see about getting tinted glasses before the bandage came off.

"I'm sorry Dr. Gish, I just…but you already left." She looked back over her shoulder. "I took your money and…" She trailed off, fishing around in her pocket, she pulled out a ten dollar bill. "I said you tipped too much, but you waved me off and I saw you walk right out the door. I was coming back to clear the table…" She kept staring at him then at Burt.

"That's ridiculous, Helen. You know I'd never tip with a ten." Eustace assessed the woman's confused face. Then he saw an opportunity. "Here Helen, sit down for a second." He guided the waitress into the booth and knelt to look her in the eyes. "I can see you're tired. Too much work? Trouble at home?"

"Um, I guess I am pretty tired. My ulcer has been acting up. Ugh, and Kimmy keeps me up to all hours wailing…" She took a drink from Eustace's half empty coffee cup nearby.

"And how are things with Jack?"

"Aw, don't get me started on that," she said thinking about the quarrel they had just the other day. She made the mistake of bringing up the idea of wanting to open her own restaurant, but Jack only got frustrated and claimed she'd never be able to hack it, that she was being delusional. What he made at the plant was enough for both of them. He didn't even like her waitressing part time but it was the only thing that got her away from her husband and baby these days.

"What if I gave you an exercise to work on? Do you think that would help?"

"Maybe?" Helen was willing to try anything. At this point she had daily fantasies of abandoning her family and running off to France to attend cooking school.

"I want you to close your eyes and picture in your stomach is a-" Eustace looked at the woman, waiting for the visual to come to him "-butcher knife."

"A butcher knife?" Helen looked at him, confused.

"Yes, a butcher knife, a nice thick heavy one. Whenever you feel overwhelmed or tired, or you doubt yourself, I want you to picture that knife cutting out those pieces, those things that are holding you back from your passions. Do you think you can do that for me, Helen?"

Helen nodded, thinking about it. "I'll give it a try, Dr. Gish. Thank you."

"What is this, therapy? Hey, Helen, get your butt up. Table 1 is ready," Louise called from the kitchen.

"Shit," Helen jumped to her feet. "Thank you Dr.

Gish," she said again.

"Wonderful. Good luck, dear. Let me know if I can help further," he said, turning back to Burt with a wide grin. "I really think this TV thing is a great idea, Burt. Probably the best idea you've ever had. Did you see that? The look of willingness in her eye? Ha." Eustace smoothed his hair back. "Get that TV schedule or whatever. This is going to be ground-breaking, count on it."

"Hey buddy, you do know it's only local access, right? We'll have a few dozen viewers at most, depending on the time slot, which I'm still not sure about," Burt was trying to tell his friend. But Eustace wasn't listening. All of his pages, the steps, were already being written.

All he had to do was have them pressed on film, and printed up, then get them out there. Shit, he was going right up there with Freud. No more teaching bourgeoisie brats. Not to mention he'd be like a god-king among men whose women were driving them up the wall.

Eustace daydreamed on his walk across campus. He'd enter any room to a chorus of applause. Men would slap him on the back as he passed. "Let's have a drink," the dean of Harvard would say. They'd oust that hack Skinner and give Eustace his office. Women would fawn over him, making Ada insanely jealous. Hopefully, she wouldn't get drunk and cause a scene. Eustace pictured Ada and another housewife yanking on each other's hair as they rolled across the lush lawn of the country club while everyone looked on.

"He must be some kind of man," they'd whisper seeing the two women fight over him.

"No one understands the female mind like Dr. Gish," another would swoon and look his way. "He's a best-selling author, teaches at Harvard, *and* has his own TV program."

Yeah, the women would want him, the men would want to be him.

"That was a funny thing at the diner, huh? Do you have a twin running around we don't know about?" Burt tried to joke, but he couldn't get the image of the shaken waitress out of his mind. He felt the same bafflement when he saw his friend walk by, completely oblivious to his name being called.

Burt had watched the man leave the diner and head past the window. He would have bet his life on it that it was his colleague. Maybe slightly thinner and better groomed, but still it was Eustace. Yet Eustace claimed up and down it wasn't. It would be a strange thing to lie about.

"Funny?" Eustace looked at Burt, "Funny how? There are troubled women everywhere. I'm not surprised."

"What? No, I mean about how she thought she saw you leave. Same thing happened to me. Remember I told you about it." They paused outside of the AV building.

Eustace gave Burt a chilling look, the shadows from the trees cut across his face making him look like he was two pieces held together by that dirty white bandage. "I must just have one of those faces."

"Uh, maybe."

Then Eustace broke out into a wide grin again, "Or maybe you're just drinking too much these days, huh?" Eustace slapped Burt a little too hard on the back.

Burt forced a weak laugh. "Ha, yeah, could be… Well, speak soon. I know the girls want to get together this week or the next."

"Sounds good. See ya later, Burt." Eustace said as he walked away. He had no time for small talk. He could feel things changing, Now it was his mission to help reunite others, and you can bet he'd do it ten times better than that hippie woo-woo Swami Motherfucker or that simpleton Skinner. He was going to heal the fractured minds of women everywhere.

+++

Ada wasn't around when Eustace got home. The house was quiet. Eustace poked his head in the dining room, Ada had been working on her wall mural. She'd finished the other side of his body, and began filling in the lines so they were thicker, bolder, making his image really stick out on the mauve background.

The windows were all open, letting in a crisp breeze that carried a hint of lake water and cut grass. Sitting in the middle of the living room was a heap of lumpy trash bags, throw pillows, photographs, plus an end table and assorted knick-knacks.

"Ada?" Eustace called. He paused at the bottom of the stairs, listening. He thought he heard a moan, even gasping… Eustace began up the steps, hoping Ada hadn't gotten herself so drunk she was getting sick in the bathroom. He'd never get any dinner out of her if she was tanked. It would be a frozen TV dinner or Chinese take-out, not the type of thing a man should eat after having such a magnificent break-through.

"Oh, oh…harder…"

Eustace paused in the hallway, hearing not only his wife's ragged gasps but a deeper voice that echoed after. It grunted and mumbled as Ada laughed and obeyed, begging for more of whatever she was getting.

Cautiously, Eustace stepped across the carpet and rested his hand on the doorknob. Ada was fucking someone in the bedroom and it wasn't him.

He pushed the door open so he could see a small slice of the room. Two figures as naked as the day they were born were on the bed. Ada was on her hands and knees taking it from the man in the back. She was too busy to notice the door open, but her male companion looked up at Eustace as he thrust into his wife.

The look on the other's face was almost bored, but it cracked a crooked grin when it saw there was an audience. Eustace quickly stepped back and closed the door, plastering himself against the wall. He looked around, he was standing in the hallway. So how was he also in the bedroom fucking Ada to within an inch of her life? Out of morbid curiosity Eustace wanted to peek again, but he was too scared at what he'd see. Was this the figure from the diner, from the supermarket? The one Annaleece was referring too?

A minute later the door opened, he heard a giggle from Ada. "I'll be right back," It said and walked out. It looked at Eustace as it passed, It's one good eye meeting his. Eustace stood there a second unsure how to respond. Should he go confront Ada or the man with his face? Should he just sneak out and pretend he was just getting home?

Eustace watched the Other head down the stairs. A minute later the front door quietly shut. "Stash?" Ada called from the bedroom. Eustace took a deep breath and stepped into the open doorway.

"Ada," he said.

"Stash? Why are you dressed? I thought we were going to…you know, again..." She sounded like a shy school girl. Eustace was disgusted. Her hair was all mussed, her cheeks red, and the room smelled like body fluids.

"Take a bath, Ada. I have some work to do tonight." he said, walking past her pouting face into the adjoining demolished bathroom. He closed the door and sat on the edge of the tub, staring into the narrow hole, feeling the blackness would birth step 3 of his new method before dawn.

6.

Ada couldn't believe Stash was going to be on TV. She couldn't stop beaming. Everything was finally happening. She was really getting into the flow of her art, the portrait of Stash coming along better than she could have ever hoped for.

"It's your three selves," she explained when her husband asked why she painted him looking so fucked up.

"You know how I feel about modern art," he told Ada.

"Your Ego, Superego, and the Id. You're always going on about them. So I thought why not give the painting a little extra dimension? You know, so there was more than just your face in there. When a creative eye looks at you this is what it sees. It's up to the artist to peel back reality and expose the underbelly." Ada ranted on gesturing back and forth from the painting to her husband. "Besides you could say it was inspired not just by you, but by Freud. You love Freud!"

"You changed my glasses. You can't see either of my eyes now." Eustace observed.

In order for Burt to agree to make a television program Eustace had to ditch the bandage and cover up the eye so as not to offend delicate housewives who may potentially watch his show. So in turn Eustace had Ada paint over the left lens with thick black paint.

"This is the real you and all of the others, Eustace! Trust me, I have a vision! And it's all because you!" Ada shouted, exasperated that her square husband couldn't get it. "Just trust me. Now, that's not what you're wearing to dinner is it?"

"What do you mean? It's just Burt and Joann, not the queen of England." Eustace looked at his tweed blazer, white button down shirt and brown slacks.

"You just look so…beige." Ada said, who had taken to wearing long caftans and chunky jewelry she bought last week from a shop on campus.

"At least I don't look like a damn gypsy, Ada. Have you seen yourself?" Eustace thought Ada was taking this creative thing a little far. Maybe her healed mind was crazier than her fractured one. It was affecting her appearance and he didn't like it. *Some birds should just stay in the cage,* he thought.

"*This* is how artists dress, Stash." The timer in the kitchen buzzed. "Oh fiddlesticks, the casserole." Ada dashed into the other room to save the food that Eustace suspected was already burned.

Eustace sighed and continued looking at the overlapping portrait of himself. The lines were messy and he looked more like a Rorschach test than a man. "Damn shame," he muttered, taking his drink and stepping through the kitchen and out onto the back patio.

The evening was warm. Burt and Jo were coming over for dinner. They were going to talk about the TV spot

Burt had finally secured for Eustace. Eustace was swallowing his excitement, this was how it all began. This small TV spot would reach hundreds, and after six episodes, journalists and publishers would come running wanting to know how he helped so many women in such a short period. He'd have to take a sabbatical from work next year for the book tour.

Eustace looked back through the patio door at Ada bustling around in the kitchen. There was no way he could take Ada on the tour. She would ruin everything talking about her art nonsense. But perhaps once she finished all of the steps in his new program she'd mellow some, get a grip, and stop dressing like a witch. She didn't even bother pinning up her hair, but let it ripple all around her like a blonde haze. It was embarrassing. She was acting like she was a child raised by a vagabond, not a mature woman of means.

This program had to help her, otherwise what would people think when they finally saw her? Because let's face it, he didn't have an attic to lock her in like in the old days. *Pity*, Eustace thought. And putting her away in an institution would look just as bad. *He couldn't even help his own wife,* his critics would say. No, everything would be FINE.

"Set the macaroni salad out," Ada said, handing him the orange Pyrex bowl. Eustace took it but continued glaring at Ada. *Fuck, she could ruin everything with her nonsense*, he thought.

Ada had only just finished step 3, telling off her uppity sister and severing ties with her alcoholic mother who kept telling her to leave her husband and just come home already. And of course she was excited about step 4, all she had to do was focus on herself and her silly painting.

Once she completed that he was sure she'd run out of steam and by the end of step six all would be well. If not, Eustace figured he'd just have to grind up some sedatives whenever they had an important engagement, no one would have to know.

"What?" Ada lingered a moment, finally catching her husband's eye.

"Hm? Oh, nothing darling." Eustace knew there was no point going on about those god awful frocks and gaudy cheap jewelry. If Ada wanted to look like her Aunt Carol then there wasn't much he could do.

The doorbell rang, interrupting the tense silence between husband and wife. "Are you going to answer that door Ada, or do you expect me to do that too?" Eustace asked, turning away to set down the macaroni salad on the patio table. The pink squares of salami Ada had stirred in were disturbing to him. Everything else in the salad was soft and round and a natural color, all but the Salami. It looked raw and pink. It reminded him of his raw eye socket for a second. As if Ada had scraped up the pink and white goo he'd flung down the sewage hole in the bathroom and stirred it into the salad.

"Hey buddy! How ya doing?" Burt's overly boisterous tone was getting on Eustace's nerves but he couldn't alienate the man, he was getting Eustace a prime spot on public access. It was an opportunity Eustace couldn't afford to squander, not when he was so close to finally getting some of the recognition he deserved. But he decided it was mostly always like that with geniuses.

People just overlooked them out of sheer ignorance, and only recognized the greatness once it slapped them in the face. Eustace grinned thinking about how he couldn't wait to slap all the doubters and naysayers.

"Drink, Burt?" Eustace asked, walking over to the patio cart.

"Ugh, yeah," Burt unfolded in a chair, letting his pudge roll over his navy trousers. Eustace looked at him, waiting. "Oh sorry, buddy. Why not make it a gimlet, eh?"

"Sure thing Burt." Eustace thought cocktails were for women and drank his whiskey straight like a man.

The women chattered away inside about Ada's painting ambitions. But Eustace knew eventually they would wander outside He was right. No sooner had he put the gimlet in Burt's hands was the patio filled with flapping sandals and flowing gauze.

"You too, huh?" Eustace assessed Joann's massive hoop earrings, her candy blue head scarf and long draping gown covered with an obnoxious paisley print.

"Me too, what?" Joann kinda laughed and took a seat next to her husband.

"Nothing, Jo. He's just grumpy. He works too much." Ada sat down. Now all three of them were staring at Eustace. "Stash? Are you gonna sit?" Ada narrowed her eyes and Eustace knew it was inevitable, he was going to have to spend the next several hours with these people.

As he sat there sipping his Wild Turkey and smoking, thinking about the hole in the floor, the endless potential of the bathroom, of his program, he grew more and more irritated. He just wanted to work, not sit here like shit on a log doing nothing. "Did you figure out a time slot yet, Burt?" Eustace blurted out.

"Stash, that was rude. Jo was telling a story." Ada chided him like a toddler.

"What?" Eustace looked at Joann who had to shift her eyes away from his gaze.

"No, it's fine Ada. I was done anyway." She took a quick sip of her cocktail and looked at Burt, giving him a little nudge.

"The time slot, well, yeah, I'm afraid the best I could do is 1am on a Thursday."

That was not what Eustace wanted to hear. "What the fuck is that Burt?!" The doctor shouted. "You said it was going to be a prime spot! One fucking AM? Who the fuck is going to want to self-realize at one in the goddamn morning? You promised me 1pm, prime housewife watching time!"

Burt cleared his throat, "Now buddy, look, I know, but-"

"Don't give me that 'buddy' bullshit! Do you understand how serious this work is? How many people like her and her," Eustace gestured to the wives, "it's going to help?"

Joann's eye's looked like they were going to bulge out of her head. When Burt saw her staring he knew he had to stand up for himself. She was always telling him he was a pushover and that was a major turn off. She liked alpha males. Men who took charge, and Burt really wanted to get under her brassiere tonight. She'd never let him if he skulked out of here like a beaten dog.

"Now look here, Eustace." Burt slammed his glass on the table, making the dishes quake. "The head of the station doesn't want some boring talk show during prime viewing hours."

"Boring?!" Eustace sputtered.

"Trust me, 'boring' is a nice way of putting it. Come on buddy, 1am ain't so bad. Maybe you can help a few insomniacs. I mean all the other stations are off the air at that time. The only reason we're still on is because the students all need to get their projects done. We need the extra hours so they can have something to add to their portfolios. So if you're not going to fill the spot, I'll have to find someone who will. And that's just how it is." Burt really hoped Eustace didn't punch him.

"I oughta cut your goddamn tongue out of your head."

"Stash!"

"Ah!"

"Excuse me?" Burt stared in disbelief while the

women gasped.

Eustace took a deep breath and slammed down the rest of his whiskey. *You'll just have to make do. You can deal with it later,* his wise inner self told him. So Eustace forced a grin and sat down.

There was dead silence save for the tweeting of birds overhead. Eustace took out another cigarette and lit it, then laughed. It was a sharp laugh that didn't make any-one feel better. But a minute later Burt joined in, urging Joann to as well. Ada followed a moment later. Eustace's booming cackle nearly drowned out the brittle laughter of the company.

"I'm just joking with you Burt. Just kidding around." Eustace assured him.

"That's a good one, you, uh, got me there bud-dy…." Burt said.

"Let's eat, I'm starving." Eustace said, clapping his hands together making everyone jump. That was some-thing everyone could agree on. Food. When in doubt eat lots and lots of food.

+++

As Ada washed the dishes she heard her husband whistling in his study, his typewriter clacking away. He had claimed his book was almost finished, and production on his TV spot began on Friday afternoon. She should have been happy. After all, a husband's success was a wife's success, but she was troubled nonetheless. Troubled not just from the awkward dinner and her husband's manic moods that floated from ecstasy, to paranoia, to flat out rage, but there was something else.

It was only a few days ago that it had dawned on her how strange she'd been feeling. She was tired, more so than usual. She had been painting a lot, so that could be it. But also she had an endless appetite, hunger would strike and there was no ignoring it. It felt as if her stomach was turning inside out, and even if she'd eaten an hour earlier she had to eat more, more, more!

Tonight at dinner was the perfect example. She'd eaten twice the amount of macaroni salad as she should have, now she felt the mayo seeping out of her pores. When it was time to serve dessert, Ada made sure to cut herself an extra large slice of Joann's lime Jell-O and cottage cheese pineapple salad cake. Thankfully, everyone was on edge from her husband's outburst and probably assumed her extra portions were related to stress. But Ada knew it was something else. She felt the fluttering deep within, her bird was nervous.

Instinctively, she placed her hand on her womb and looked down. It couldn't be, could it? After all these years? The thought stunned her so much that she dropped the dish she was drying. Even as it splintered on the tile she couldn't help but simply watch it, feeling detached from reality.

"Ada? Ada what's that?" Eustace yelled from the office.

"Huh? Nothing dear," she responded, finally kneeling to pick up the pieces of china. She dumped the whole thing in the trash, left the rest of the dishes soaking in the sink and went upstairs. She carefully closed the bathroom door so Stash wouldn't hear. It seemed every time she was in the bathroom he insisted on getting in there.

Ada knelt on the tile and looked down into the damp black hole where the toilet once sat. "Is it possible?" she asked. She continued staring as if waiting for a response. When she placed her face on the sub-flooring, Ada thought she could hear laughter way down inside the bowels of the house. She moved closer, listening intently. No, it wasn't laughter, but close, a baby and it was crying. "Oh," Ada sat up, clutching her middle. A baby, her baby.

"Are you in there again? Ada!" Eustace banged on the door.

Quickly, Ada got to her feet and pulled open the door.

Eustace observed his wife. "You're bleeding," he said, gesturing to her lower arm. Ada looked down to see a cut weeping red.

"I don't know how…"

"Have you been lying on the floor, Ada? Have you been near the hole again? I told you about that. That's not for you." Eustace said, stepping towards her, so she had no choice but to move backwards into the small room.

"No, I was just going to take a bath," she began.

"The water is turned off," Eustace told her knowingly. Both husband and wife looked down at the opening in the floor.

"Is it? I suppose I didn't realize," Ada said, taking the opportunity to push past Stash and into the bedroom.

"Hm?" he asked, not really paying attention to her anymore. What was his wife doing with the hole in the bathroom? He knew what it had to offer him, a man who was ascending, but his wife? To what purpose could such a thing serve the simple creature?

Eustace closed the door behind him, clicking over the lock. He went to the mirror and looked into the large triangle piece that still clung to the frame. Beside him stood the other. The one who he was slowly becoming.

At first this troubled Eustace, the other shadow self, running around fucking his wife (and probably his student) then lurking in diners, pretending to be Eustace himself. But after that night in the hallway when it passed by him and went out the door like a draft, Eustace was sure he knew what was going on. He got that feeling once more, like he was finally connecting with an old friend and he shouldn't be afraid. What was meant to happen, would.

Eustace sat his glasses aside and peered at his two selves, one reflection looked back at him, the other kept his face turned away, looking forward into the dark of the hallway behind. As Eustace got deeper into his process

the door numbers had changed from 1 to 2 to 3 and upwards, so now he stood outside of door 5, soon he'd be to
door 6 and after that? Once a common man, soon to be a
superman, beyond society and values, creating his own reality through simply existing. *Goddamn right.*

+++

Ada chewed on her nails, waiting for Eustace to
leave. She had a doctor's appointment that morning to
get a pregnancy test. She didn't want to say anything if it
turned out to be nothing. Her husband had been so hot
and cold lately, one moment making love to her like a savage beast, the next acting as if it had never happened.
Though, she figured, if there was ever a time she could
have fallen pregnant, it was that night.

Stash hadn't fucked her like that since…ever. And
neither of them were even drunk. He just came in and took
her, ripping off her dress and kicking his pants aside, like
he didn't even care if they got wrinkled. He said her painting had turned him on. That she was so beautiful when
she was creative and free. His methods were working, she
was doing an amazing job. She was an inspiration to wom-
en everywhere, and soon she'd be free like him. Together
they'd heal the world.

But after that he hadn't fucked her since and only

complained about the evolution of the portrait on the dining room wall, her clothing, her hair, everything. It seemed like there wasn't anything she could do right.

The coat closet door clicked open and shut. Ada walked into the front hallway as Stash was slipping in his jacket. "Have a good day," she told him, sipping what remained of her coffee.

"I doubt it. I have to waste all morning telling these moronic students they better get their shit together because almost all of them failed my pop quiz on Tuesday. I would have expected this kind of thing from my female students, they are after all quite distracted most of the time. But the men? What the fuck is going on with the youth today, Ada? I tell ya, fucking idiots. It's probably best that we never had children; they would have grown up to be complete brats. I'm almost sure of it." Eustace finished buttoning up his blazer and looked at his wife.

"Ada? Oh, come on, I didn't mean it like that. It wouldn't have been our fault. It's society, the way it coddles these kids' fragile egos. Most of them think they should pass simply because they bothered to come to class!"

Ada thought about pitching her coffee mug directly at her husband's forehead. She just wanted him to shut the hell up already. She looked at Stash a moment longer, that smug look on his face, and she decided to do just that.

"I would have been an amazing mother!" She chucked the white cup at her husband's face.

It felt like slow motion, the cup missed Eustace and

broke against the wall, splattering the remains of coffee all over the shoulder and sleeve of her husband's jacket.

"ADA!?" Eustace wasn't shocked his wife had thrown her mug, she'd thrown plenty of things at him in the past. But that was before… Before she went into the hospital and got the shocks and Chlorpromazine. Eustace briefly feared she was having a relapse. Fuck, what was he going to do with an broken wife? It was just as he worried before, if he couldn't help her, how would anyone else take him seriously?

He moved towards Ada, who stood there in her orange kimono and tousled morning hair. She even had the audacity to smile. "What's the matter Stash? Am I being too irrational for you? I thought you wanted me to be free!?" She laughed, turning to leave, but Eustace grabbed her arm and yanked her back into the hallway so she hit the wall. Her head drummed against the wallpaper, making the picture frames knock.

"What the fuck am I doing to do with you?" His sour coffee breath made Ada want to gag.

"What am I going to do with you?" she asked in defiance. Ada was getting tired of this, tired of men in general. When Ada thought about the future, all she saw now was her living in a cute bungalow with Joann. That was the only thing that really got her wet these days, the thought of curvy, bubbly, soft Joann going down between her thighs. Now that looked like freedom.

At first the thoughts troubled her, but then she realized they had always been there. Every time she spoke or saw her friend she realized how happy she was. A man had never made her feel like that. With Joann, Ada wanted to experience endless pleasures, create, and embrace life!

Oftentimes as Ada painted, she found herself lost in the thoughts of Joann. The two of them running off together, painting, and living every day to the fullest in some big city where their love would be accepted. Joann often mentioned how fabulous New York was, how beautiful Paris had been. Ada had never been to either, but realized now that she wanted to. She wanted to go everywhere with Joann, if only Joann wanted her too.

Ada hadn't worked up the courage to make a move yet, but felt it would have to be soon. Pregnant or not Stash was really getting on her nerves. Now he was slamming her against the wall and growling in her face. Something he never used to do.

Maybe it was the stress from work, or writing his new book, but whatever it was Ada didn't care. She had to do something drastic if she ever truly wanted to find herself.

"Are you listening, Ada, *dear*?"

Her eyelids fluttered as she met her husband's one naked eye, the other hid behind the shaded black lens. He was so proud of that nasty old wound, refusing to go to a doctor or even acknowledge how disturbing it was that he'd gouged out his own eye for reasons he wouldn't go into.

"I have a doctor's appointment, I need to get ready.

Have a nice day at work." Her voice was so eerily calm that Eustace released her and stepped back.

"An appointment? What's wrong now?" Eustace asked, waiting to hear about how Ada thought she had damn uterine cancer like that twit from the soap opera she watched.

"I think I'm pregnant," she said, for once very sure of herself.

Eustace wasn't expecting her to say that. "That's impossible, Ada. Don't waste your time."

"Impossible? How could you say that?"

"Because I can't even remember the last time I fucked you," her husband said. Nothing about this woman aroused him anymore. She was weak and frivolous, and the painting he initially thought was a good idea turned out to be a mess, just like every other hobby she attempted.

"I can't believe you just said that. What about a couple of weeks ago? What was that? Because I vividly recall you ramming your throbbing erection into my wet pussy, remember?!"

"Ada, watch your mouth." Eustace felt his cheeks beginning to burn. He thought about that night, when he finally came face to face with his other half. How he'd seen some part of himself penetrating his wife while Ada howled like an alley cat in heat, begging for it.

"My mouth? Remember how good it felt when I put my mouth on…" she trailed off enjoying her husband's discomfort. "…your cock? How it made me sopping wet and you just had to put it in and-"

Eustace reached out and slapped his wife hard with an open palm. "You imagined it, Ada." he told her, his expression daring her to go on.

Instead of crying or acting shocked, Ada kept the wry grin on her face as the spot where he hit her burned. "Hm, I guess. We'll see what the doctor has to say. Have a nice day, *dear*…" She turned away and floated upstairs, feeling really good. She'd decided that she'd had enough. Now her own husband wouldn't even admit to fucking her, it was over. After the doctor's appointment she was going to see Joann and tell her everything. Just the thought of her voluptuous friend made her hotter than a man ever could.

+++

Eustace was pissed at his wife and couldn't help recalling the scene again and again as he walked to work, crossed campus and entered the Physics and Astronomy building. It annoyed Eustace that psychology didn't get its own building, but instead was stuck in the very back of the sciences, like an embarrassing step-child you didn't want anyone to notice.

How could Ada do this to me. Why can't she just fucking hold it together? What the hell am I going to do with her? His thoughts chased each other around and around. It almost felt like his method was making her worse. He'd caught her in his study the other night going through his pages, claiming she was ready for step 5. Eustace had to wrestle the damn paper from her hands. "I'll tell you when you're ready," he said. Finally Ada stomped off and went to bed.

The delicate building blocks of his life that he had stacked together over the years felt like they could come tumbling down at any moment. From the outside he looked great, a nice house by the lake, a wife, a good job, and soon to be a best-selling book and TV program. But if anyone looked closer who knows what they'd see. Him, shoving his infertile wife against the wall and slapping her face. Eustace might have felt a little bad, but Ada was so insane she didn't even flinch, but seemed to enjoy it.

Eustace felt something grab his shoulder. He shoved the thing against the wall, for a second seeing Ada, then himself, then some moron's face. "D-d-doctor Gish?" it squeaked.

"Whoa buddy, what are you doing there?" Eustace turned from the moron's face to Burt's who was just walking through the doors. Eustace turned back to the kid in front of him, his hand continuing to grip the guy's throat.

Burt put a calm hand on Eustace's arm. Reluctantly, the doctor let his friend guide his arm down to his side, releasing the student who gagged and nearly fell over.

"What's going on?" Burt asked, turning from Eustace to the kid.

"Nothing, he surprised me, that's all. I'm under a lot of stress and this jerk just grabs me out of nowhere." Eustace looked at the kid, daring him to disagree.

"I'm sorry Dr. Gish, I just had a question about the quiz."

"See, buddy, he just had a question. Everything okay here?" Burt asked again.

"Yes," the kid squeaked, forgetting his question and rushing away into the lecture hall.

His fear made Eustace grin, he liked that. That's what he wanted from Ada. That's the only thing that got him going these days. Like when he saw Annaleece get struck by that car, the heat he felt rush through him, it was intoxicating. "So everything's okay?"

Eustace turned back to his friend, "Oh you're still here?" he asked, annoyed that Burt was ruining this great feeling of savage control.

Burt cleared his throat. His friend was turning into a real asshole lately. "I just wanted to say we're clear for taping at the end of the week. Be there by 1:30, okay? Unless you'd rather just stick to the book and not bother with this whole TV thing. I can see what you mean, it's a lame duck of a spot…"

Burt was hoping to convince his friend to back out then they could just leave the spot blank. He'd find another project for his students to work on. A nice wholesome documentary about the ducks at the pond, or maybe the Spiffy

Baking Company. He could take them on a walking tour of the plant, now that would be a good film. They could split it up into a weekly series no problem.

"Nonsense." Eustace leaned in close, "I'm telling you, this stuff I've been working on is gold. I don't need a prime spot, all I need is a few people to see it and the rest will come running. Word of mouth, it's the best advertising a person can have. And I know this is good. Just you wait. After six episodes you'll be begging me for more." Eustace told him.

Burt couldn't decide if his friend was conceited or delusional but either way he shrugged, "Sure thing. See you then, buddy. Just wanted to let you know about the time."

Eustace looked at his watch, he was running late. "Sounds great, see you at lunch?" Eustace asked, walking towards his class at the end of the hall. A few stray students rushed past, relieved to see their professor was late as well.

"Uh, not today. Joann packed me something. I've got a lot of grading to catch up on." It was an obvious lie. Burt and Joann had talked about distancing themselves from Eustace and Ada after the cook-out incident.

Joann thought they had 'bad vibes' and Burt couldn't help but agree. It was too bad, he'd known Eustace and Ada since they moved here.

People change Burt. I mean Ada is okay. But Eustace? He's a real bastard to you. Burt thought about his wife's words, and she was right. After this TV project it was done, that was it, the end.

Eustace didn't seem to care one way or another. He waved his friend off and slammed the door to the lecture hall, leaving Burt to realize that damn, he was late too.

+++

Ada wasn't pregnant, the doctor assured her. She also didn't have uterine cancer but he could refer her to a specialist if she was really worried. "I was just so sure I was," Ada said.

"The mind can play cruel tricks on you," her doctor said, patting her knee.

"I suppose. I've felt so different the past few weeks that when the idea dawned on me I could have sworn I felt movement right here," she said, pressing her hand to her lower abdomen.

"Probably just your digestion." Her doctor gave her a knowing look. Ada's shoulders sagged, only half believing him. But then again, if it *was* true then there really was nothing stopping her from leaving her husband for her soulmate, Jo. Now she knew why her Aunt Carol was always so happy despite everyone feeling bad for her that she was unmarried ceramics teacher and a lesbian.

"I can increase the dosage for your tranquilizers," her doctor offered.

But Ada was done feeling sorry for herself. She jumped off the bed and threw off her gown. The doctor had seen it all before. "No, I'm fine. I swear. I've got somewhere I need to be. Thank you doctor," she said, wiggling her frock down over her spindly frame and grabbing her handbag. "Have a nice day," she said before rushing past the secretary.

From the window her doctor watched Ada jog out to her teal Bel Air. A moment later she tore out of the parking lot and onto the road. "Everything okay, doctor?" the secretary asked.

"Call Mrs. Gish's husband please. I'd like to speak to him," the doctor said, going into his office. There was something about Mrs. Gish's behavior that worried the doctor. Whenever it concerned the womb there was a chance of hysteria. The doctor was sure Ada was on the brink, if not halfway there. It was best if her husband was prepared to put her back into the hands of the clinic if need be.

+++

Ada pulled around the curve of the cul-de-sac so quickly her car went up on the curb. She didn't care. She parked it on the sidewalk and figured that was good enough. Ada wasn't expecting to be here long. She was sure Jo felt the same as her, and soon they'd be throwing suitcases into the back of the Bel Air and blazing a trail for themselves, free from the shadows of their dull husbands and empty days.

Ada took a deep breath before pushing the door bell. She waited, then pushed it again, and again and again until - "Ada! Goodness, what's going on?" Joann stood before her in a fitted blue blouse, a starched white skirt, and red strappy heels. The morning light framed her body and made her look like a goddess.

"I have to speak with you Jo." Ada was nervous but excited. She followed Joann into the living room and sat down on the curved rose gold sectional.

"Can I get you some coffee?" Joann asked.

"No, no, just come sit down." Ada patted the cushion beside her, eager to tell her friend everything. The idea of it was making her heart hum and her panties wet. When Joann sat, Ada noticed the line that went down Jo's shirt, the outline of her ripe breasts. And the crease where her friend folded her legs. Ada wanted to open those legs and devour her.

"You're blushing Ada, good god, what is it?" Joann asked, moving closer. Despite wanting to part ways with Eustace, Joann didn't mind Ada. She was nice and funny and always around whenever Jo needed someone to make herself feel better.

"I had the worst fight with Stash this morning," she began.

"Oh, I'm sorry, Ada dear." Joann put her hand on

Ada's to comfort her.

"But it doesn't matter. That's all we do is fight lately, and this morning I realized I've had enough."

"Really?" Joann was impressed, she didn't think Ada believed in divorce.

"Yes. And I'm tired of living a lie."

"A lie? Whatever do you mean?" Joann asked.

"I mean fuck my family, fuck Stash, fuck convention! I want to be free, Jo, and I want you to be free with me!" Ada didn't wait for her friend to respond, she pressed her mouth over Joann's luscious red lips and wiggled her tongue in, finally tasting her friend.

It took Joann a second to realize what was happening. It wasn't the first time she'd kissed a woman, but she'd never expected this from Catholic Ada.

Still it felt nice, Jo thought, relaxing and finally giving Ada a kiss back. "I want to kiss you deeper," Ada said, pulling away.

"Do you?" Joann was impressed, watching Ada crawl to her knees and push Jo's legs apart. Joann leaned back as Ada kissed her way down Joann's torso to her lap, finally pressing her face to the beautiful gash between her legs. Ada could smell Jo's desire. She carefully opened Jo's pants, tugging them down while Joann giggled, letting her legs fall open.

Ada didn't waste any time, kissing Jo's cunt through her silken panties and pressing her nose in deep, inhaling her female musk. Joann begged for Ada to remove

her panties and kiss her. Ada finally did just that, faithful-
ly licking, running her tongue up and down Jo's gash till her
friend's thighs grew soft and her mounting cries ceased a
mere five minutes later.

"Run away with me Jo," Ada said looking up at
her friend, now lover. Joann's head was resting along the
back of the sofa, gazing at the ceiling. She'd torn open her
blouse and one of her breasts was exposed, moving up
and down as Joann's chest heaved.

"Ha, I'm sorry, what?" Joann finally looked down at
Ada. Her mouth was red, and she had a manic look in her
eye that said she was serious.

"Run away?" Jo pushed herself up. Ada stood,
smoothing her skirt. "Ada what are you talking about?" The
light-hearted pleasure Joann felt just seconds ago was
quickly dissipating.

"You and me, away from Stash away from Burt.
Let's get the hell out of here. Let's go to…Paris! You always talk about how amazing it is. We can paint and just
live. People will accept couples like us there. Come on, Jo.
Let's go!" Ada was rushing around, hands in the air, more
than ready to throw caution to the wind. Joann was sure
Ada was having some kind of manic episode.

"Ada, we can't." Joann tried to say before Ada
swung around and rushed towards her, grabbing Jo's
wrists and pulling her hands up to her lips, kissing along
Joann's knuckles, then stopping at her gold wedding band.

"Why not? Why can't we Jo?" Ada said, staring,

almost transfixed by the small diamond sparkling in the morning sun.

"I love Burt. He's my husband. I can't just run off with you. Come on, Ada. We were just having a little fun, that's all. Nothing more than that. Girls do it all the time. It doesn't mean we're all about to leave our husbands over it." Joann tried to tell her.

Ada dropped Jo's hands and looked at her friend. The spark of excitement that lit up her blue eyes a moment ago was dead. "A little fun? I love you Jo, and I know you love me." Ada said in all seriousness. This wasn't going how she thought it would. In fact, she was 100% sure things were going to happen according to plan. She saw the scene play out, imaging it in her head while she sat in the bath night after night. Jo wanted her just as bad as Ada wanted her, she was so sure.

"You're messing everything up, *Jo*." Ada took a step towards Joann as the woman tried to back away.

"I think you need to leave now, Ada. Do you want me to call Burt or Stash to come and help you. I think you're-"

"Oh, just shut-up. Why does everyone think I need help all the time?! I told you, I love you, Jo. Now say it back! Say it!" Why couldn't anything ever go right?

"No, Ada." Jo tried to sound firm when in reality she was trying to think of a way out of this situation. *Stay calm,* she told herself. First things first, she had to put her underwear back on. Then she had to calm Ada down and get to the phone.

"What are you doing?" Ada asked when Joann bent down to locate her panties.

"What does it look like, Ada? Christ, I'm putting on my clothes." Joann was irritated. Why did this kind of thing always happen to her? This was the third woman to get a crush on her in two years.

"Stop it. Don't put your panties back on, Jo. Stop!" Ada demanded. Before Jo knew it Ada was shoving her backward onto the carpet and climbing on top of her.

"What are you? Stop! Stop it, Ada!" Jo struggled beneath her friend's weight as Ada ripped and clawed at Jo's face.

"Do you think you can use me like that? Am I some sort of sidekick? I'm good enough to give you head but not good enough to run away with? Huh?!" Ada was screeching while Joann fought back. "Stop, stop moving, Jo."

The two women tumbled on the carpet, Joann trying to get away to put her underwear on while Ada was trying to stop her. In the struggle Jo rammed her forehead into the corner of the coffee table. "Fuck," Joann groaned, still trying to crawl away. She felt a hot bump beginning to grow on her face. Ada used this opportunity to take off her heel.

"One last chance, Jo. Do you love me?" Ada asked from above her.

"Huh? Ada…" Jo's brain was muddled with pain. She turned as Ada brought the heel down into the soft socket of her eye.

When Ada saw what she'd done, she fell back, watching the scene. It didn't seem real. Joann howled like a cottontail being torn apart while blood gushed out of the wound. Ada's shoe was stuck in Jo's face.

"Oh my god, oh my god, oh my god." Joann was huffing as she sat up. With shaking hands she touched the heel protruding from her face. "Ada, help me," her voice trembled.

"I said I loved you."

"Please, ADA!" Joann screamed with the last of her strength, yet Ada stood there, satisfaction growing on her lips. This was exciting. Ada wondered what would happen next.

"The phone, I need to c-call for help…" Joann was thinking out loud. She needed an ambulance, she needed Burt. She needed to do something before she blacked out.

Joann began crawling across the floor. She decided somewhere in her brain fog to go down the stairs to the front hall, that was the closest telephone.

"Jo, where are you going now?" Ada asked, following the woman. "I really want to talk about this. Please Jo, I'm sorry okay."

Jo pulled herself up so she was leaning on the banister. She wanted to look Ada right in the eye. "Fuck you, Ada. You're fucking crazy," she spit. Ada couldn't believe her best friend in the whole world just said such a thing. This was the end, Ada was sure of it.

Ada pushed Jo as hard as she could, sending the semi-naked woman down the wooden steps before smacking into the nearby wall.

It looked kinda funny in a way, a woman tumbling down the stairs like that. But the fun didn't last. Joann flopped over and looked up at the ceiling, the heel pushed further in than before.

Ada slowly walked down the stairs and stood over her friend, looking at her stained blouse and quivering face. She couldn't believe this was the woman she was so in love with only ten minutes ago. Joann was always so strong and outspoken, now she was a sobbing, hateful mess.

When Ada poked her with the top of her toe Joann groaned but didn't try to move away. "I think I need… a doctor," Joann gasped through the wet veil that coated her face. "Ada…" she said, begging.

When Ada was satisfied Jo wasn't going anywhere, she went back up the stairs to the sitting room. The clock reminded her it was almost time for her stories. She had to see what happened to Bert.

Joann groaned, but the TV did a great job of covering the death rattle. "Shut-up," Ada said, flipping open the box of chocolates Joann kept nearby. "My you're quite the little piggy," Ada said, trying to pick between the left behind coconut and the half chewed caramel that someone had put back. *Probably Burt*, thought Ada, Joann would never do such a thing.

It wasn't until the commercial for Spiffy muffin mix came on that Ada realized how late it had gotten. "Jo, I should probably get home. Do you want help getting to the bathroom or anything? Stash just put a bandage over his eye, he was fine. I'll need my shoe back though… Jo?" Ada wandered barefoot down the stairs. Joann was pretty much where she left her, crunched against the wall looking bloody and ridiculous. "Jo? I'm sorry everything got so out of hand." Ada paused, looking at her friend.

"I don't blame you for being mad. Jo?" Ada bent down and twisted the heel of the shoe out of her friend's face, but Joann didn't stir. The wet sucking noise as Ada removed the heel was disturbing, but it was the stench that really hit her. "Oh Jo, did you need to go to the bathroom?" Ada couldn't help but smile, but Jo didn't twitch.

"Fiddlesticks, we can't leave you here like this. Burt will get so mad. Um…" Ada tried to think about what she should do. She'd only seen a dead body once, and that was her grandmother who had died huddled in the coat closet (she had dementia). It was days before anyone found the old lady who must have forgotten how doorknobs worked. Stash would be mad too, but he might be a little more understanding than Burt. "Okay, I guess I'm taking you home," Ada said. "Let me just pull the car around."

Ada walked outside and brought the car into the attached garage, closing the door behind her. She dragged the drink cart from the front room and draped Joann over the top. "My goodness you're heavy," Ada said, rolling

Joann out to the garage. Ada walked back in to retrieve her bloody shoe and noticed the mess. Joann would be embarrassed if Burt came home to find the house was a disaster.

Quickly Ada straightened the sitting room, located a few towels and bleach to wipe down the floor. Finally she pulled the rug over the parts of carpet with heavy blood staining. She returned the drink car to its place beside the sofa, and had a final look around. "Oh, silly me," Ada rushed to pick up Jo's underwear. Burt surely would have had questions if he came home and found his wife's underthings laying around.

Of course, Ada thought. She went into the bedroom, and took a suitcase out of the closet, picking out a few pieces of Joann's clothing that she'd always wanted.

"All set," she said, climbing into the Bel Air, backing out of the garage and down the driveway.

In two minutes she was home and parked in her own garage. "You just stay in there. I'll talk to Stash when he gets home," she told Jo's remains.

What a long strange day it had been, Ada thought, wandering up the stairs with Jo's suitcase and her bloody heel. She cleaned the shoe off in the guest bath and took off her own dress to soak. Blood stains were a bitch to get out if you didn't soak the garment right away. She turned sideways in the mirror, assessing her stomach. It looked to be slightly bulged, there had to be something in there, there just had to be, Ada thought.

Next, Ada went through Jo's suitcase and brought out an emerald house dress. It was a little loose in the bust area, but Ada could always take that in later. She was hanging up the rest of the clothing in her closet when she heard the front door open and shut. "Stash?" she called down the stairs.

Her husband looked up, he was surprised to see his wife hadn't sulked in her bathrobe all day. In fact she looked more vibrant than she had in years. "Ada?"

"Stash, I have to tell you something," she said, coming down to meet him in the hallway.

"I already spoke to Doctor Halflinger about your visit this morning. I know you're not pregnant."

"No Stash, that's not it," Ada cut in.

"I told you not to waste everyone's time on that nonsense."

"Stash!" Ada's shrill cry cut through Eustace's flat words.

"There's no need to shout, Ada. Why don't we go sit down for a second?" He tried to guide his wife away from the front door.

"That's not what this is about. Stash, I… ugh, Joann is in the Bel Air." Ada said as Eustace tried to push her into the living room, but he paused to look at her.

"Why is Jo out in the car?"

"Because she…" Ada thought it best to leave out the lesbian stuff. "She… I… We had a misunderstanding and she fell down the stairs. I didn't think it was that bad but she died." Ada tossed her hands in the air as if there was nothing to be done. "I didn't want Burt to get mad so I cleaned everything up and now Jo's in the trunk. I'm sorry," she whined.

Eustace rubbed his temples, all he wanted was dinner, but forget about that. "Let's go have a look then, Ada. Can't you just for once stay out of trouble?" He followed his wife out to the garage.

After the phone call with Dr. Halflinger this afternoon, both he and Eustace were convinced Ada was in the throes of another episode. However, what to do about it was something of a debate.

Eustace assured the doctor to leave it to him. The last thing he needed was his wife in the nuthouse while he was trying to launch his new career. He had to keep whatever was wrong with Ada under wraps. Maybe he'd drop an extra tranquilizer into her cocktail after this. That would calm her down so he could think for five damn seconds.

Ada held her breath as her husband popped open the trunk. "Is it bad?" she asked, not wanting to see the look of annoyance on her husband's face or that gory hole in her friend's head. She heard Stash exhale. "Ada," he said over her babbling.

"Just tell me, Stash. Just say it! Say it! I'm a killer, oh Jesus, forgive me…"

"Ada, shut-up. There's nothing in here you daft cow."

Ada turned and looked at the empty trunk, "No. No,

that's impossible." But it was, her eyes were telling her so. "Where is… Stash, she was here, I swear it. Oh my goodness, she must have gotten out. Maybe she wasn't really dead. Shit, she could be calling the cops right now!"

"Just calm down Ada. There's an easy way to fix this," her husband assured her. Eustace wanted to lose his mind and put her in the trunk, but knew he couldn't do that… yet.

"There is?" Ada asked, looking at her husband. She let Eustace guide her back into the living room where he sat her on the sofa. He picked up the phone, calmly dialing a number.

"Who are you-"

"Sh," Eustace told her, letting the phone ring. "Yeah, hi Burt it's Eustace. No, everything is fine. I was just wondering if Jo was around?" There was silence while Ada tugged on Eustace's shirt sleeve like a child.

"Stash, no."

But he ignored her, like always. "Hello, *Joann*," he emphasized, looking at Ada who fell silent. "Yup, one second. Ada wants to say hello." He handed the receiver to Ada.

"No, no," she whispered, but he shoved it at her anyway. Finally, she took it and attempted to collect herself, "Jo?" she finally said into the mouthpiece. The whole scene ended with yelling, crying and Ada throwing the phone receiver down into its cradle.

"Everything alright? Now you know Jo is alive and

well, yes?" Eustace asked in a calm voice.

"Yes," Ada said through her tears. "Oh, Stash the stuff she said…" Ada wept. She was so confused. She didn't know what was real anymore and what wasn't.

"She's crazy," was all she could get out in between sharp quick inhalations. "I'm going to take a bath…" she finally said.

Ada got up, climbed the stairs, and paused outside of the guest bath before going on through the bedroom to the other bath. She let her clothing fall around her feet, not caring if they got dirt on them. Ada sunk down deep into the tub and laid her head back, there that felt better. She listened to the bells coming from the sewer drain, they were soothing and sounded like the singing bowls of Swami.

+++

"She's insane," Jo said, hanging up the phone.

"You wanna tell me what happened?" Burt asked, sipping his drink, looking at his disheveled wife.

"I don't even know. Ada burst in here this afternoon saying she loved me and wanted to run off to Paris together. And I told her no, she was being irrational, and then… She just lost it!" Joann took a slug of her martini. "I'll tell ya

Burt, I've never seen anything like it. After five straight minutes of her yelling, she took off her shoe and just chucked it at me. It hit me square in the forehead." Joann gestured to the lump on face before going on, "So I ran into the bathroom and locked the door. I sat there for almost two goddamn hours. When I came out she was gone, the living room was rearranged, and I think she stole the basket of laundry I had sitting on the bed for some reason." Jo scratched her head. "Now just what do you suppose that's all about? Who steals someone's laundry?"

"Hell if I know," said Burt. "I think they're both heading for a breakdown. I mean look at Stash's eye. What's going on there? I asked him about it and he said it happened when he was renovating the bathroom. Acted like it was no big deal. I mean it's his fucking eye!" Burt took another drink.

"Renovating, ha! Ada showed me the 'renovation' last week. It's just a demolished bathroom with broken mirror everywhere. But Ada acted like it was the most beautiful thing. I don't know Burt, something about it gave me the creeps." Joann shook her head recalling the dreamy look Ada got when she motioned to the sewage hole.

"Something weird is definitely going on…" Burt mused. "After this project with Eustace is done, maybe we should think about moving across town, eh? Give us all a little space."

"Move? Do you really think that's necessary?" Joann asked, sitting beside her husband.

"Well, I don't want those looney tunes within two feet of the baby, do you?" Burt placed a hand on Joann's womb. "You haven't told Ada?"

"Of course not. Especially after today. I think it's just better to keep it to ourselves for now." She gave Burt a knowing look and he silently agreed. The couple clinked their cocktail glasses together in celebration of the pending arrival of their first child, but also in continual gratitude that they weren't Stash and Ada.

7.

"I might be pregnant. Maybe I should get a second opinion" Ada told Eustace. She couldn't understand why he wasn't more excited.

Eustace usually never smoked in bed, but tonight he was making an exception. It had been a really long day followed by a really long month. He was so close to bringing his genius into fruition that he could taste it. But between Burt, his wife and her friend, plus all of his needy students who wouldn't get out of his face with their preschool questions, he was at his wits end.

"You're not pregnant, Ada. Dr. Halflinger assured me there was no way in hell you're pregnant. But he did propose you may be perimenopausal and should make an appointment for that. Maybe a good dose of hormones would help level you out."

Ada glared at her husband. "That's bullshit! What would you know about it? I know what I'm talking about, and I *know* there's something in there."

"Uh-huh. Just like how you knew aliens were real? Or that Swami Asshole had all the answers? It's madness, Ada. Can't you hear yourself?"

"Swami Nhincomhpoda was right! If it wasn't for him you would have never gotten your book written!"

"That's bullshit. Take that back."

"No. Admit it, Stash. If I hadn't taken you to that class you never would have learned how to connect with your higher self. Swami showed you the door, you know it's true." She jabbed her finger in the air.

"Like hell I do." Eustace couldn't believe she truly thought that. His methods were all his. If Ada started a rumor that he'd ripped off a hippie cult leader everything would be over before it began.

"At least I'm not so full of myself that I can't give credit where credit is due," she said.

"And what's that supposed to mean? Do you think I should dedicate my work to that charlatan?"

"All I'm saying, Stash, is that I acknowledge the spirits and my true self. I see it reflected in my work and I have amazing masters to thank for that. I am grateful for the bounty that the universe has bestowed upon me."

"You sound like a nut job, Ada." Eustace snubbed out his cigarette. The husband and wife said nothing more, each knowing the other was stubborn and there was no point.

Ada, in her mind, was so sure she was going to have a brilliant painting career, and perhaps a baby as well. With every brush stroke she became more and more enlightened to the mysteries of the universe and all the doorways that were open to her. She simply needed the courage to go through them.

Now she knew why spirit mediums and gurus were so humble. Spirit or the universe or God or whatever you wanted to call it had chosen them. And now Ada was sure the higher power had chosen her. Who knows? Maybe she was channeling some great ancient god or some higher aspect of herself that existed on another plane. Whatever it was, Ada had never felt such purpose and inspiration.

She just knew she was going to be a great mother, *the best* mother. Journalists would rave when they came to interview her about her work, that she was also a mother *and* a wife, not to mention beautiful and perfectly sane.

Ada, with curlers pressing into her scalp, her face mask smelling like a toxic sea, knew all the sacrifices she was making, would have to make, were all going to be worth it.

Eustace had a tough time drifting off to sleep. While for once he felt his life's mission was clear, he didn't know what the fuck he was going to do about Ada.

Just don't worry about that, yet, Eustace told himself. *Just think about the good things. You're on the right path, you're the next big thing.*

As soon as the show was taped, the book was done, it would only be a matter of time before publishers and journalists were banging on his door wanting to know all about his theories. He'd go on for hours and they'd beg for more, wanting to know how he, a humble psychology professor, developed such insight into the female psyche, a place no man dared to visit.

"I've only got myself to thank," Eustace would say. And it was true, it was all him. He could quit his stupid teaching job. People would come to his lectures because they actually wanted to, not because they were hoping for an easy grade.

With heavy eyes the doctor finally drifted off. In the stuffy dim hallway Eustace looked at himself standing inside door number 5. He knew without a doubt what his other half was trying to tell him, sacrifices would have to be made, and he knew it would all be worth it.

+++

"It'll look fine," Burt said, trying to keep everyone calm. Eustace was a wreck, he was chain smoking while the students were still struggling to frame the scene and get the lighting right.

Eustace thought he should have a better sound stage, but the best they could do was the basement studio that was mostly filled with outdated equipment, boxes, and broken chairs.

"Andrea, why don't you pull down that screen to shield the cabinets back there. And uh, Doug, move those boxes over there." Burt instructed his students. Eustace watched them scurrying like ants. He couldn't believe he'd have to trust these amateurs with his greatest work. Eustace didn't think he'd be so nervous, but damn it, his hands were shaking, he was sweating through his jacket.

"This is wrong, all wrong!" Eustace glared at the trash heap all around him.

"Dr. Gish, please calm down," Burt said, glaring at his sort-of friend. "We're doing the best we can. I told you how it was going to be."

"A basement I can deal with, but Christ! These kids are amateurs. Look at him!" Eustace glared at Noah trying to center a chair over a large X on the floor. "He can't even center a piece of furniture over a damn X. I'll be surprised if he can even point the camera in my general direction." Eustace raked his fingers through his hair, causing it to fall forward in his face. He dropped his cigarette butt on the floor and went to light another.

"How about you do that outside?" Burt suggested, "We'll finish setting up. Then we'll see where we're at. This is just uh, preproduction, it's supposed to be a bit chaotic."

"Right," Eustace glared at Burt for a second, seeing blood falling over his face like a crimson veil. Eustace continued staring at Burt a moment longer than either of the men were comfortable with.

"I'll be back in ten," Eustace said. Maybe he just needed some fresh air. He didn't sleep well last night, then woke up to Ada playing Indian rock n' roll records and throwing paint against the wall at 5am.

Eustace turned to walk down the long basement corridor. It was a short walk, a right hand turn, up a few steps to the exit door. The doctor heard the footsteps before he saw the man they belonged to. He saw his per-

fect mirror self walking towards him, calm and confident as
ever.

The two men came to stand before each other in
the hallway. Eustace finally acknowledged his great self
with a tight nod. Then in silent agreement, Eustace knew
what was going to happen. His higher self would deal with
this filming bullshit, while Eustace went home to do something about his wife.

A moment later Eustace walked out into the day,
knowing Dr. Gish was walking into the studio, and no matter how unprofessional or junky the set was, it would be
perfect. Eustace had been blind to the fact that the physical didn't matter, it was all about inside, the invisible pieces of a person that surgery couldn't locate - the spirit, the
imagination, feelings, all the selves people had but never
saw.

Eustace hated to think the swami was right though,
to some extent, at least. But still, he couldn't help but laugh
on his walk home. Men like that would never be as great
as he was going to be because they were held back by the
constraints they placed on themselves. They'd never do
the really hard stuff, the messy stuff, to surpass others and
ascend to a greater place of true healing.

There was no doubt in his mind, he had manifested
his mirror self in the flesh, did he not? The two were blend-
ing into one. It was scary at first, but after looking into the
man's eye, seeing himself reflected back, Eustace had no
doubt he was truly going to be a superman.

+++

The music was so loud Ada didn't hear her husband come through the front door. He stood in the dining room doorway glaring at her back. Ada, Ada, Ada, his darling wife Ada. He remembered her first breakdown that occurred after her fourth miscarriage. She spent nearly two weeks in a hypo-manic state rearranging furniture, cutting her hair, and drinking endless cups of coffee long into the night. She wanted to learn how to draft blueprints so she could have their old house knocked down and a new one erected in the Prairie School style, despite having no previous knowledge of architecture or drafting.

"I want a one bedroom house, no big dining room, why would we ever need that?" She ranted, playing with a ruler, drawing a large rectangle with a few lines, before declaring it done.

"Where are the measurements, Ada?" Eustace asked, staring at her drawing.

"The what?" She looked from the paper to her husband before crying. Soon after she stopped bathing and laid around all day staring out the window at the lake. After another several weeks of that, Eustace decided to commit her after she bit him one day.

Now here she was doing the same thing all over

153

again. Making a fool out of herself with the neighbors, dragging him to all of those hippie classes, forming these grand ideas that she was pregnant and would become a great artist. Not to mention all of her delusions like killing Jo, seeing him around town when he was clearly at work, and bathing in a tub that had no water. It had been four days since she'd taken an actual bath with running water, but Ada didn't seem to notice her stench.

Sacrifices have to be made. Eustace heard his higher self's words loud and clear, ringing like a bell in his head.

Eustace walked into the living room and switched off the record player, throwing the house into a sudden and heavy silence.

"Hello?" he heard Ada's voice ask. Then came the noise of her hopping down off her chair, the hushed sound of her stocking feet moving over the carpeting. She jumped when she came around the corner and saw Eustace stand-ing next to the turntable.

"Stash! Good God, you gave me a fright. What in the hell are you doing?"

"Why? Don't you want me here, Ada? What are you up to that's so secret?" he asked, sliding his hands into his pockets.

"What? I was painting Stash. But you, you were go-ing to start recording your show today. What happened?"

"Nothing. Consider it done."

"Oh, really? How did it go?" Both were engaged in

a seemingly normal conversation, yet both felt it was leading them somewhere far away. Eustace knew he had to get
Ada out of the way, and Ada knew Eustace was going to
try and stifle her genius. There was tension building, and
both could taste it. Would Ada try to run or defend herself?
Or would Eustace grab her and knock her out first?

"It went fine. I saw someone you might be familiar
with." He was thinking about his shadow self.

"Oh, who? Burt?" She snuffed at the name. She
was done with those backstabbers.

"I saw the Other clearly for the first time in my
whole life. And he looked right back," Eustace said.

"The Other?"

"My higher self, he was there. You know him, the
one with the slick hair and straight posture. The one you
fucked and told yourself was me."

"Stash, what the hell are you talking about?" Ada
shook her head as if the very idea hurt her brain. Eustace
should have known it would be too much for her to handle.

"I know you're familiar with him. Otherwise why
would you spend so much time upstairs in that bathroom?"

"Our bathroom? Maybe I was taking a bath." Ada
said, wondering if her husband was trying to gaslight her.

"That water isn't turned on, Ada. There's only a hole
in the floor and a broken medicine cabinet. There's nothing in there for you. We both know that. Now come on, look
at yourself." Eustace began moving closer to his wife, who
continued to stand in the doorway, her body becoming rig-

id.

Ada knew this was it. "Look, Stash, I know how all this seems. But maybe I truly am connecting with some higher self, just like you. Maybe we can be great together. I'm *not* crazy," she emphasized. "In fact, oddly enough, I feel better today than I have in…since I can remember." She tried to laugh to break up her tight words.

Ada should have known this was going to happen after reading her husband's outline for step 5. She should have poisoned Stash's meatloaf when she had the chance. Now however this was going to end, it would be bloody.

"Ada," he said, pausing a moment. "You're covered in paint, and you've convinced yourself that your rock hard womb could actually grow life."

"It is," she insisted, finally moving from her perch by the door and backing away as he came closer. *A weapon, a weapon*, she was going to need something… She thought about the Civil War sword on the wall over the fireplace in Stash's study. It had belonged to a long dead relative that had fought for the Union. Or she could dodge across the hall to the kitchen and grab a knife out of the drawer.

"Ada, are you thinking about stabbing me?" Eustace spoke as if he were talking about the weather.

"Stash, just come see the painting. I really think once you see the full picture then-"

"Ada, don't you understand I have things to do? I don't have time to screw around with your artsy nonsense!

People need me to help them and you're just getting in the way!" He couldn't listen to her damn chatter any longer. He had reached the end.

Eustace lunged for her, but Ada away slipped inches from his fingers. "Stash!" She ran across to the kitchen. Searching in the drawer she realized she hadn't done dishes in days, all the knives were dirty and lay wet and slippery at the bottom of the sink beneath pots and plates.

She hurried on through the dining room, and into Stash's study. "Ada, stop," he commanded, coming in after her, blocking the door. He followed her eyes to the sword over the mantle. "Ada, be serious now." He came closer wanting to end this silliness as soon as possible.

"No, stop!" Ada yelled, clawing at Eustace as he tried to force her down to the ground, finally giving into the urge to twist her head off.

So when the heavy *thunk!* hit him, it took a second to realize Ada had clubbed him with the bust of Freud he kept on his desk.

"Ada..." he said as everything went fuzzy.

"Sacrifices have to be made, Stash." She placed a protective hand on her midsection. "How will I ever get well if I don't do the work?"

"What? Ada... Ada..." he trailed off, feeling a warm bloom open on the side of his head. Eustace fought against the black falling over his vision, but in the end he closed his eye, letting himself drift into a sea of sand. He felt something had gone very wrong here.

PART II: ADA

8.

Ada didn't know what to do with Stash. Usually when she got into these messes it was Stash who helped her sort things out. Like when she thought she'd killed Joann, it was her husband she'd turned to for help. But now it was just her with a bird pecking at her brain. Maybe it wasn't a sparrow or finch at all but a woodpecker, digging around searching for mites and bugs, creating more harm than good.

But perhaps it was better this way. After all, her husband wasn't the man she married. It was like he was two different people, and she never knew which one was going to show up. The atomic belittling husband or the caring, understanding thinker who would sit patiently for hours talking through her worries and fears, then end it with a good roll in the sack. This man whose blood was soaking into the carpet wasn't Stash, he was an impostor, she just knew it.

Ada remembered reading about something like this in one of Swami Nhincomhpoda's books, how we as a society are severed from our primal, pure self. That wound can manifest severe illness, including cancer or madness. So it was very important to do the work. It was something many tried to do but went insane in the process.

Ada recalled sitting over there near the window,

reading that line over and over again, *...many tried to do but went insane in the process.* It frightened her to think such a thing was possible, that the path to Swami's truth could either set you free or send you down a spiral of which you could never escape. Either way, when it came to The End, you could only be one thing or the other - enlightened or crazy.

Ada wanted to be enlightened, but poor Stash had clearly gone mad.

With her husband unconscious, Ada wondered, what next? He was still breathing a little bit, and she really didn't want to hear him yell at her when he woke-up. She figured it would just be best to get rid of him. It could only help things by this point.

Out on the patio Ada shoved everything off the drink cart. The shrill sound of glass hitting the gray slate was loud in the otherwise quiet night. She pushed the drink cart into the office and pulled her husband onto the lower tray. Ada thought she heard him groan as she knocked the corner of the cart on the wall, jerking him back and forth.

"Sh," she said. It felt good to tell her husband to be quiet for a change. She moved him through the house to the kitchen, rolling him off onto the terracotta tiles. She had to keep this contained, that made things a little easier. This incident would not stretch beyond the frame of this house. That made her feel she could handle it.

"Okay, Stash, or whoever you are, I guess it's the chest freezer for you." Ada said. She opened up the drawer that held cooking utensils like ladles, cheese slicers, and measuring spoons. She located the heavy steel meat tenderizer. "Hold still, this should only take one hit."

She couldn't fathom the thought of just stabbing the man over and over again, it was too brutal. But knocking him in the head she could do. It would be just like when she went to her uncle's slaughterhouse outside of Stockton when she was a little girl.

All the men there simply knocked the cow upside the head before they knew what hit them. Well, usually it was just one blow, if the man was good and strong. The sound the cow made when it took several hits would never leave her ears, the groaning and fright of the thing.

"Don't worry, you won't feel a thing," she promised. Her husband failed to move. She brought the meat hammer down to meet his head. "Stash?" Ada asked after a moment.

She got down on her hands and knees and put a finger in front of his nose. She thought she felt a breeze. *Damn, okay,* she thought. Ada planted another blow, further caving in Eustace's head. The pulpy soft insides began to swell out amongst the cracked bone shell.

She looked at the red gore but remained steady, figuring there was no sense making a big scene about it. It was done. She didn't think she'd be able to do it, but she had, and knew that the sacrifice was well worth it.

Her husband, her inspiration… and her doubter. *Such a tragedy,* she thought. If anyone had asked Ada twenty years ago to imagine her life now, she never would have conceived of anything so exciting.

Despite all of these worries bubbling up, she was feeling better, more free, than ever! In fact, she was so wrapped up in her own success she never gave a second thought to Eustace's mention of the Other.

Ada plugged in the underutilized GE electric meat knife, "Damn it," she said, tugging on the chord. It was too short, forcing Ada to pause and locate an extension before getting down to business.

It was a bloody mess by the time she was done. Now her husband was wrapped and packed into the large freezer in the garage; organs, bones and all. At least she wouldn't have to be going to the store any time soon.

Upstairs, Ada got undressed and slipped down into the bathtub, staring at the wall of smashed tile, dust, and plaster. It had been a long day, she sighed, rubbing her neck.

She looked over at the sewage hole, hearing the sound of babies whimpering, bells ringing. "Soon," she whispered, closing her eyes. "Mommy's working on it." she said, patting her flat belly. Her stomach held a tuna sand- wich from lunch plus two cocktails, a cookie, some paint she had chewed off a brush, and a small bit of Eustace's blood she had sampled out of sheer curiosity (it was too salty for her taste).

Ada felt good despite everything. There were 6 steps in total according to the sewage hole, and she was in the middle of step 5. The End was upon her and it made her happy.

+++

"That's not a baby," he said. Ada opened her eyes to see the smeared image of Eustace hovering over her.

"But-" she began, annoyed and somewhat defensive that Stash would not leave her in peace. *Just let me have my damn baby,* she thought, silently cursing the phantom.

"You'll never have a baby, Ada, because your body is filled with sickness in the form of nerves, trauma, and boredom. Why don't you come out of the bath and we'll talk about it?"

Ada knew she should be scared but in truth she felt relief, just another thing that proved she was sane, there *were* two Eustace's lurking around. She just hoped this one would be more helpful than the last one, because her freezer was full. The wicked little thought made Ada smile.

"But I wanted a baby," Ada finally said.

"I didn't say you couldn't have a baby," the new Eustace said, leaning closer and talking in her ear so it was barely a whisper. "But just be aware, what you carry inside of you is not a infant. You can have anything you want. You've removed nearly all the obstacles that were stopping you from achieving greatness, Ada. If you want to be a painter or a mother, you will be."

"I see," Ada said, leaning back against the better version of her husband. Her new husband was right about one thing, this was totally the one who had fucked her. It was lean and strong and totally in tune with a woman's needs. Unlike Stash, who just put it in and pulled it out without ever bothering to stimulate her clitoris.

"Hey, did you hear about Joann down the street?" Eustace asked her, setting the brush aside and beginning to massage Ada's shoulders.

"Ugh, what about her? She's insane." Ada was sick of Joann.

"I hear she's pregnant. About four months now."

"What!?" Ada's eyes snapped open and she felt wound up again. "*Her*?" Ada was disgusted. "Why the hell does that lying bitch get a baby and I don't? She pretended she loved me then just threw me away like trash!" Ada turned around to glare at Eustace. "Why are you telling me this?"

Eustace remained calm, unbothered by her outburst. "Oh, I was just thinking about what a good mother you would be and what a horrible mother old Jo will be. She's so self-involved, so unrealized. Imagine what she'll do to a child?" Eustace said, going back to massaging Ada's tense shoulders.

Ada chewed on her nail, thinking. "She doesn't deserve that baby," she said more to herself than her new husband.

"Do you think do you?"

Ada didn't even have to think about it, "Yes!" Her declaration was firm, she'd never felt so sure of anything.

"That's wonderful, honey. You deserve to have everything you want. If you feel being a mother is your path then I think you should follow it and see where it leads. Don't let anyone keep you from happiness, Ada."

She turned to kiss him, but new Eustace stopped her. "It's been a long day, honey. Let's put you to bed, hm?"

"Okay," she said, allowing him to help her lie down before covering her with the quilt.

"There we go, all snug and comfy?" The shadow asked.

Ada thought she could see his eye burning in the dark. When she continued to stare at him he asked, "Everything alright Ada, honey?"

"Yes," she said. "I love talking to you, Stash, or whoever you are. It's strange, I know you're not my husband but still it feels like… talking to an old friend. Thank you for helping me," she said.

"See you soon." He turned to leave.

"But Stash," she asked, half asleep.

"Hm?" he paused in the doorway. Ada opened her eyes and noted the strange sight of a shadow casting a shadow.

"If I'm not pregnant, how will I get a baby?"

"We'll talk about that tomorrow. Now close those

eyes, go to sleep," he told her.

"Good night, Stash." Ada said, drifting off. She hadn't realized how tired she was till that moment.

+++

When the sun came through the windows, Ada laid there for a moment, feeling the warm light on her face. For a brief second she feared yesterday was a dream. That she'd wake up and grumpy Stash would be lying next to her like a cold stone.

She stretched out her arm, allowing her hand to caress the place Stash usually slept. His pillow was untouched, he hadn't been to bed. *That's because he's in the freezer,* Ada assured herself. She thought she'd be sadder, but the idea of being free made her unbelievably happy.

The smell of breakfast, the sound of pans in the kitchen, drifted up to the bedroom. It was strange to smell coffee since for as long as Ada could recall she was the only one who would make it.

Even when she had her miscarriages and was put up in bed, Stash couldn't be bothered. She had to peel herself out of bed to get coffee or go without. Stash claimed he had too much work to do to take time off. He was up and at work the next morning, leaving Ada to cry into the pillow all day.

So it felt surreal to Ada walking into the kitchen and seeing the thing, her "husband," making toast and scrambled eggs with fresh coffee. "Hello?" she said, still half asleep and confused.

"Oh, good morning, honey. I thought after such a trying day yesterday, you'd like a reprieve from breakfast. Hey, how about we go out to the club tonight? It's been ages since we've dined there," he said, coming over to usher Ada to the kitchen table.

"Really?" Ada asked. She looked over her breakfast, and damn it if it didn't look like the best thing she'd ever seen. "This looks delicious, Stash," she said, taking a drink of coffee. "Is this from the freezer?" She gestured to the strips of meat on her plate.

Eustace laughed, "I carved it myself. And yes, I'm serious about dinner. We're going out tonight," he told her. She smiled and both ate, reading over the paper. Finally, Stash stood up and began clearing the table casually as if this were an everyday occurrence. "So are you going to paint today?" he inquired, pouring yellow soap into the sink.

"I'm not sure. Have you looked at it lately? What do you think?" Ada asked, taking her coffee and wandering into the former dining room to look at her work, now dried from yesterday's session. There was a smear of dried blood where her former husband's head banged into the corner of the wall last night.

Eustace joined her a few moments later. "It's coming along brilliantly. It says so much about who you are as a woman," he said. "And I really like the color choice right there." The new Eustace pointed out the small dried stain. "Don't worry," Eustace said, sensing Ada's worry, "It'll be our little secret." Both smiled.

"So you really think it expresses me as an artist? *Really*? Hm…" Ada continued to stare at her work. Her new husband really saw all that, so it must be true.

"Of course. It shows you are a deeply realized, spiritual being. You see beyond the mundane. It's something many people don't even realize they are blind to. They spend their lives stumbling along wondering what they should be doing? Or what's wrong with them? But you, Ada, you're special. Just look at this brilliant piece. And soon you're going to be a mother… Imagine being fulfilled on every level. Can you see it?"

Ada stared ahead at the swirl of color on the wall, picturing it. "I can. I can see all the way to the end, and it's so beautiful." She felt herself glowing from the inside out.

Suddenly, all she wanted to do was rip off the new Stash's clothes and have her way with him. She reached for him, but he grabbed her wrist and held it firm.

"No, Ada, not now. I have to get to class. Remember I'll be a little late because of filming. But be ready at 8, and we'll go to the club. How's that sound, honey? Good?" he said, releasing her hand.

Ada nodded, "Yes, of course, Stash. I'll work really

hard. Do you think after dinner we could talk about what's inside of me?" she asked, the idea still weighing on her.

"What's that now?"

"You said there's no baby inside of me, so what is it?" she asked.

Eustace thought for a moment, before saying, "Well, that's a complicated question but to make it easy let's say it's You."

"What..? Me?" Ada placed her hand on her stomach.

"Yes, Ada, it's the last piece of You."

Ada continued looking down at her midsection.

"Ada?"

She looked up at him standing in the kitchen doorway. "Yes?"

"Have a nice day. You don't have to be afraid anymore. Hey, I know what might help."

"What?" she asked, trying to focus on Eustace and not the idea of a ghost-self inside her womb.

"Why not get rid of some of this clutter? That might calm you down a little bit," he suggested.

"Clutter?" she asked, looking around.

"Yes, honey, clutter. Take for instance that dining table and chairs over there. It's a constant reminder of something that will never come to pass. Why keep it? It only prevents you from moving forward," he said.

Ada thought about it, maybe he was right. "Okay, yeah, why not?" Her new husband gave her a quick peck on the cheek on his way out the door. Life was beautiful.

After Eustace left Ada spent the next hour wandering around staring at remnants of the life that never came to be no matter how much she tried. She was living someone else's dream, thinking for the longest time it was hers.

Unlike a lot of Ada's girlfriends that went to college to major in finding a husband, Ada actually wanted some sort of career. She'd learned early on that when her mind wasn't occupied with a project it tended to wander to places she didn't want it to go. And of course Ada also wanted children, a loving spouse, but it seemed she took a wrong turn and ended up here instead. Childless, friendless, no career, and a dead husband. Well, sort of, she did have this new, better version of Stash, who saw her potential and actually took her seriously.

"Maybe it's not so bad…" she murmured, taking in her surroundings. She had a nice house by the lake with large windows and high ceilings, trees and a fair size lawn, plus a Bel Air sitting in the driveway. Once she got rid of the dining set she'd have a real studio.

Ada figured even if she had taken a wrong turn and stumbled into this reality by accident, now was her chance to right that cosmic mistake.

In the dining room, Ada began pulling the chairs two at a time through the doorway and out the glass slider to the patio. She tossed them out into the grass letting them bounce and roll a little ways before stopping part way down the hill.

Ada continued to do this until the entire set was sitting in a heap on the grass. Now she had a choice, burn it or throw it in the lake? It seemed like it would create a nice healthy fire, so she figured she might as well add some more fuel to the flames and get rid of a bunch of stuff at once.

"This is for my books!" Ada said, throwing her dead husband's clothing among the discarded furniture. She also collected several boxes of papers, framed photos, his favorite chair, his stupid framed PhD, and the bust of Freud she used to smash his brains in.

Slowly the fire began licking at the furniture, growing in size. "Fuck you Freud!" Ada sang, seeing the bust blackening as the pages curled to ash.

"Ada?"

Ada quickly turned around to see Joann walking along the shoreline towards her yard. "What are you doing?" her neighbor asked as she came closer, looking from the flaming pile of household belongings to the woman she used to call a friend.

"I'm just doing some spring cleaning, that's all." Ada said, bathing in the hot satisfaction of fire.

"Uh-huh," Jo said in disbelief. "It looks a little big, doesn't it?" she asked, concerned the wind might shift and blow hot ash towards her property only a few doors down. "Did you get a permit for this?" she finally asked.

Ada had to pull her eyes away from the inferno. She liked to think she was burning the veil away, and only now was she truly seeing the world. Everything looked brighter, funner, and more fulfilling than ever before. Was it soul evolving? Or perhaps it was the fact that her husband was dead? Whatever it was, Ada was sure it somehow led back to the swami's teachings, and the appearance of this wonderful star-being wearing Stash's face.

"I don't need a permit to burn rubbish in my own yard," Ada said. She felt as if she were moving beyond society, above it. Rules and laws were for people who didn't know their own mind, but she felt rock steady and confident in her choices.

"But you do," Jo insisted, watching the flames grow higher, the heat intensifying. She felt as if she were standing just outside the gates of hell. When she looked up the slope towards the house she saw broken bottles strewn along the patio, the doors wide open, curtains blowing out the windows. Inside it looked dark and empty, giving Joann a shiver that told her to forget about her clothes and just leave.

"Where's Stash?" she asked, feeling a tad of worry for her former-friend. The woman obviously needed help.

"Working. He actually has goals in life, unlike some lay-about husbands," Ada said.

"Or really?" Jo knew Ada was taking a dig at Burt who liked to spend his days off lying around sunbathing or getting drunk on the boat.

"He's going to change the world, my husband." Ada beamed, her eyes wide and glassy.

"Look," Joann sighed, trying to keep her cool, "I just came by to get the laundry that you stole the other day. It had my favorite dress in it. I would like it back."

Ada looked at her for a second as if she hadn't a clue what Jo was talking about.

"My clothes," Jo said again, her patience slipping.

"I hear you're pregnant."

Joann couldn't hide the look of shock in her face. "Where did you hear that?" Jo asked, feeling uneasy. She took a step back as Ada turned her full attention to her.

"Stash told me. I suppose Burt must have let it slip. You're what? Four months now?"

"Almost five," Joann said.

"Oh, that's nice." Ada reached out a hand to touch Jo's stomach, but the woman shrunk from her touch. "Hey Jo," Ada began.

"What?" Joann was abandoning the idea of taking her clothes back.

"How early can a baby come out? Like, what's the minimum it has to cook in there? My last miscarriage was in the middle of the sixth month. It looked like a little baby then, but it was too small to live. They tried, but his lungs weren't developed enough. Do you think if you had the baby at seven months it would be able to live outside the womb?" Ada asked.

"I have no idea, Ada." Joann said. Her annoyance and anger were slipping away to a raw, creeping fear.

"Have you chosen godparents yet? Because if

something happens to you or Burt, *heaven forbid*, it would be a shame for the tiny thing to end up an orphan. You know Stash and I are always here if you need us." Ada's voice fell from manic joy to a dripping whisper as her eyes took in Joann and her midsection.

Ada couldn't believe she hadn't realized sooner. How could she have missed that slightly rounded belly? She had simply assumed Jo was eating too many chocolates in the afternoon.

"Ada, I've got to go now."

"What? No, please stay. Come in for a cup of coffee. You can see the painting. I'm really making progress on it."

"No, I'm sorry. I'm really in a bit of a rush," Joann said. "Maybe another time." The wood in the fire split, creating a loud *crack!* Making the woman jump.

"But what about your clothes? I've got them right upstairs," Ada said.

"Just get them back to me whenever you can. I've really got to go." Joann waved, rushing away across the grass.

"Bye!" Ada watched Joann scurry across the yards, finally reaching her own. "Fake cunt," Ada whispered, feeling Jo simply came by to rub her burgeoning womb in Ada's face.

Back inside, Ada marveled at the wide open space of the former dining room, now officially her studio. The floor to ceiling mural dominated the room. From the window Ada could see the fire burning her old life to cinders.

"It was never me," she affirmed out loud. She knew when the other Eustace came home he'd be impressed.

Ada spent the rest of the day chewing on her paint brushes and staring at her mural, trying to decide if it needed more ocher or not. When the wall clock in the hallway rang Ada realized it was six in the evening. "Shoot," she said, pulling the paintbrush from her mouth.

Ada had forgotten Eustace wanted to go to the club for dinner. He'd be home at eight and she hadn't even begun to dress.

Upstairs, Ada went through her closet. Everything felt outdated or seemed to fit her weird. It came down to her blue dress with gold beading or the yellow floral dress, but even those looked dull when she stood in front of the mirror.

They hung off her frame, as if they didn't even belong to her, but a stranger. A boring, mediocre, dead inside stranger. A stranger with a husband who didn't take her seriously. A stranger who had no direction and no clue who she was or what she liked. So instead she dressed for others, hoping they wouldn't notice the confusion behind her desperate smile. Just then Ada decided she had to dress for herself, society be damned!

There wasn't time to go buy anything new. It would take her at least two hours to pick a cocktail dress from a shop filled with dresses. There were just too many choices these days. Ada felt her anxiety beginning to wiggle in her mind, creating pockets of worry.

She glimpsed herself in the mirror, standing there in her peach silk slip, fidgeting with her hands like the weak little housewife she had sadly become.

"Damn it, Ada." She narrowed her eyes at her reflection, knowing somewhere deep inside she was stronger than that. Her new husband believed in her, so why couldn't she believe in herself? She didn't want to let the new Stash down, because then she'd have no one to blame but herself.

"Pull it together." Ada slapped herself hard. Upon feeling the sting on her cheek she did it again, her wedding ring scraping her lip. A fresh red crescent beaded from the shallow cut. Ada licked it and held herself upright, there she was. She saw her real self shining through, tough and resilient, like she used to be.

It was her inexperience, her older husband, her parents, and polite society that had cowed her as a young woman and made her feel unworthy of anything except housework and children. Wanting anything else was selfish and should not even be considered. If cleaning and grocery shopping couldn't satisfy you, that was on you.

Your husband's success is your success, Ada's mother often lectured when Ada complained about having to drop out of college so she had more time to host cocktail parties.

"Fuck you, mother. And fuck you too Stash!" Ada shouted, her hands wrapped in tight, angry fists. She thought about old Stash lying in pieces in the chest freezer, and she felt a surge of confidence. He always complained he didn't like frozen things. That idea made her laugh, the thought instantly perking her up.

"Now, find a dress and do your hair. Your husband will be home soon," she ordered herself. Ada tossed her two dresses aside and returned to her closet, pushing hangers along the rod, knowing there had to be something. That's when she stopped on the glaring emerald jewel tone of Joann's dress shining amongst the other drab, sensible clothing. "Dare I?" Ada muttered, taking it out and looking at it in the light.

Ada slid the pricey garment up and pushed her arms through, adjusting the neck line, and carefully pulling the narrow matching zipper up the back. She smoothed her hands over pleats, turning this way and that. She knew she didn't have time to go out and purchase a new dress, but she did have time to make a few little adjustments. Joann's bust was a bit larger, her hips a little wider, but if Ada just pulled in a few hems with a couple stitches she'd be all set.

Quickly, Ada dropped down the dress to the floor, rushing to retrieve her sewing box on the high shelf of the closet. Right away she noticed her favorite sewing needle was missing, but she didn't have time to search for it so went with one size smaller for the stitches.

"You are beautiful," she told her reflection afterward, spinning around in the mirror. She felt like a fresh spring leaf ready to unfold and bask in the upcoming season. The clock down stairs rang seven. "Blazes…" Ada pulled herself away from her new image and went into the bathroom. There she teased her hair, smoothed it and began twisting it back into an elaborate beehive. She stuck in the crystal bobby pins she normally only wore at Christmas.

At her temples she set two pin curls and sprayed the whole thing down with Aqua Net. Damn, she was glad she took the chance and bought one of those silver and pink cans. All the ladies were raving about it. Simply spray and it would hold your hair during a tornado if it came to that. *Super-Hold* the can proclaimed. "I hope so," Ada said, setting it down and smoothing down any last fly aways.

Next she turned to her make-up. All her life her mother told her less was more. "You want it to look like you're not wearing any. Unless you *want* people to assume you're a lady of the night," she remarked when she saw the pale pink lipstick Ada wanted to wear at her wedding.

But all Ada ever wanted to do was paint her face in colorful hues like the women in the movies.

Her hands shook as she carefully applied the foundation. Normally a little brown mascara and she stopped there, worried even that was too much. But on this particular evening she pulled out the ruby lipstick she'd shoplifted from the department store one day on a whim. It was hidden amongst the beige and peach tones.

Ada took a deep breath. "It's just like painting," she

told herself, steading her hand while she outlined her lips then began filling in the center, making a loud *SMACK* as she pressed them together, before blotting with a tissue.

The face that peered back at her already looked more alive than it had in decades. "Oh sweet Jesus," Ada started in awe. She couldn't believe that was her. Excited by her transformation, Ada went on to add a heavy gold eyeshadow to match, plus a little rouge on the cheeks. When she was done Ada thought she looked like a queen. "You look fucking fantastic," she told herself, never feeling more alive and real.

The moment struck her, she was self-realizing, just like the swami and new Eustace had talked about. She was mending the wounds life had inflicted upon her being. It would only be a matter of time before she would ascend with that beautiful child into her arms, becoming the interesting, perfect mother she always knew she would be. On top of all that, she'd be a world renowned painter. Her husband would become a best-selling author, maybe even more famous than the swami. Burt and Joann would be green with envy. Ada and Eustace and their new child would move into an even bigger, gaudier home on their own private lake.

Ada snorted thinking about how fantastically bright her future was, and Jo or her mother or anyone else who ever looked down on her had no idea. Or maybe they did… maybe they saw the candle flame of brilliance burning inside her and were jealous. So they used all their energy trying to passively snuff it out with unfounded fears, gas-lighting, and doubt.

Well, Ada was on to them all. The next time some-one suggested she was having a manic episode or that she should see a doctor, she was going to send them di-rectly to a frozen Hell like she did with Stash.

When she heard the front door close, Ada jumped, grabbing her white heels and hurrying down the hall.

"I'm ready," she called, coming down the stairs to meet her new husband. She wondered if he would be im-pressed with her vibrant new look.

Eustace paused, assessing the turquoise dress that was wrinkled and sat slightly crooked on Ada's lithe frame. "Why Ada, look at you," he finally said.

"What do you think? Is it too much?" she asked, spinning around in front of him.

"It's perfect. Is that Jo's dress?" he asked.

"Yes, is that okay?"

"Absolutely. I just ask because when she wore it she looked like a dying pine tree, but you look like a god-dess. You're a vision, Ada," Eustace purred, placing his hands on her shoulders while caressing her skin with his thumbs. Ada beamed, everything was happening and she was making it happen through sheer force of will.

As they were leaving, Ada noticed a small brown bag sitting on the side table. "What's that?" she asked.

But Eustace picked it up before she got to it. "That is a surprise," he told her, tucking the brown package under his arm.

+++

Everyone looked at the pair when they entered the club. Ada in her emerald dress and Eustace in his tweed blazer. People were silently assessing Ada. She looked more and more unhinged every time they saw her.

The women however were confused by the scene. They felt disbelief as the couple walked by. None of them had ever noticed how sexy Dr. Gish was.

How did a nutcase like Ada ever keep such a man? She looked as if she fell into a pile of crayons with that heavy make-up all over her face. And her dress! Her bust was not even big enough to fill it out, yet he only seemed to have eyes for her.

That evening when the women went home more than half of them would end up seducing their spouses, all the while picturing Eustace Gish, wishing he was the one pleasuring them instead of their boring old husbands.

When the vision of Dr. Gish hit their minds they rode their husbands down into the bed, orgasming harder than they had in years, if ever. *What is it about that man?* Each silently wondered afterward, smoking a cigarette while lying beside their dozing partners. Whatever it was, they wanted, *needed*, more.

Ada and Eustace took a table out on the patio. "Are you warm enough?" He offered Ada his blazer.

"No, I'm fine." She smiled at him. Old Stash never would have offered. He actually wouldn't have agreed to eat outside either. He'd say he was paying for a restaurant. If he wanted to eat outside he'd stay home and have dinner on the patio.

As they toasted each other, Eustace said, "I almost forgot your surprise." He pushed the brown paper rectangle over to Ada's side of the table.

Ada couldn't remember the last time her husband had bought her a random gift. "What is it?" She carefully unfolded the top and took out a book. "Stash," she said looking at the cover. It was a new copy of *A Familiar Face.* "But I thought you…" she trailed off looking at the hardbound edition. It was nicer than the second hand paperback she had previously.

"Ada, we both know why *he* didn't want you to have that book. *He* didn't want you to self-realize like he was. Your former husband was selfish, but don't worry, I'm here now and I support your journey," Eustace said.

It felt as if millions of sparrows were flying around in Ada's body, not in a mad rush, but in a beautiful symphony moving in time with the rhythm of the universe. "So you don't mind if I continue my studies with Swami Nhincomhpoda?"

"Continue? I'd say you've been following the path all along. Look at the way you overcame all the barriers your former husband and society put before you. You're a very impressive woman, Ada."

Ada was at a loss for words. She pressed the book to her chest, "Thank you, Stash. I love you." Ada said, feeling so loved and grateful she worried she might melt into a puddle.

"Is that my dress?!" Ada heard a shrill voice interrupting the moment. Both she and Stash looked towards the doorway to see Joann and Burt standing there, an awkward looking hostess between them.

"If you could come this way," she was saying, but Joann remained frozen despite Burt trying to take her arm and lead her away.

"It is. That's my fucking dress that *you* stole! It shouldn't even fit you." Joann yelled in disbelief. "My, my Ada, you have some nerve. You know, I almost felt sorry for you. But now, you know what?"

"Jo!" Burt cut in, trying to stop his wife from making a further scene.

"I don't know what you're talking about." Ada turned her back on Joann who continued seething in the patio doorway.

"Let's just sit down Jo, come on." Burt said, finally getting his wife to follow the seating hostess to a table over in the corner.

"This isn't over," Jo threatened as they passed by.

"Eustace," Burt gave a tight nod.

"Burt, would you like to join us?" Eustace asked, as

if nothing had just transpired between the wives.

Now it was Burt's turn to look at his friend in disbe-lief. "I don't think that would be a good idea."

"What do you mean? I think it's a fucking fabulous idea," Jo cut in.

"So do I," Ada said in a firm, cutting tone.

Burt was going to sweat through his shirt. "I think some space would do us all some good." He tried to rea-son.

"Bullshit, sit down Burt." Joann ordered, pulling out a metal patio chair and sitting down, knocking the table and rattling glasses as she arranged herself. The waitress standing nearby felt uneasy about the whole thing, but in the end took their drink orders and left it.

"Thank you, sweetheart," Eustace told the young girl. She blushed despite normally being sickened when an older man used terms of endearment like *sweetheart* or *darling.* Yuck.

"I'll… um, I'll have those drinks coming right over, I mean up…ha-ha… I'll be right back." The waitress said in between stumbling laughter. Did she feel giddy? Damn, she did. Something was going on she thought, walking away.

Joann might have felt the same if she had been focused on Ada's new Eustace rather than on the dress her former friend wore. "Tell me exactly what you're doing wearing my dress, Ada, because I can't figure it out. Are you insane or just a bitch?"

Burt cleared his throat, catching Joann's attention. He gave his head a firm shake *no.* Joann pulled her irritation in. More than anything she wanted to throw Ada over the railing of the patio and down the hill on the other side. "How about we switch to a more pleasant topic," Burt suggested, taking a drink of his water, wishing it straight vodka instead.

"Congrats on your pending arrival," Eustace said.

Neither Burt nor Joann said anything, but glared at each other, thinking the other had spilled the beans to their crazy and somewhat creepy neighbors.

"Thank you," Joann said, her voice somewhat frosty. She finally glanced at Eustace and she felt her tension begin to melt. "If you don't mind me saying, Stash, you look…nice." Joann choked on that last word. What she wanted to say was *delicious.* Jo found that she couldn't, nor did she want to, take her eyes from the alluring man sitting across from her. When Burt noticed her unflinching eye contact he took another heavy gulp of water.

"Where the hell is that damn waitress?" Burt didn't want to talk to Eustace or Ada, and his wife suddenly had a hungry look in her eye, as if she was ready to rip her clothing off.

"So Burt," Eustace finally said, like he didn't notice the heavy, wanting eyes of the restaurant's women on him, like prey in a hyena den. "How's the editing on the episode going? I think today's session was even better than the first. But I might be a little biased," Eustace said. He looked at Joann who let out a loud harsh laugh. Ada followed suit not wanting to be outdone.

Eustace gave both women a smug grin and lit a cigarette, waiting for Burt's response. But Burt was too busy looking at his wife and her googly eyes. The way she was twisting a strand of hair around her fingers and laughing like an ass disturbed him.

"Burt?" Eustace finally asked when the man failed to answer.

"Huh?" Just then the waitress delivered the cocktails. "Thank the lord," Burt said, knocking his back.

"Burt, darling, slow down." Joann said, tapping his arm.

"Whatta mean?" Burt asked, annoyed at his wife. Usually she was the one he had to tell to slow down.

"I mean, we're at a nice restaurant. You don't see Stash getting shitfaced do you? I mean, really." She laughed, looking towards Eustace who winked.

By this time Burt wanted to punch the guy right in his good eye. The thought of smashing those glasses into his face sounded like a dream.

"How about I'll stop drinking when you stop ogling Eustace like a wanton?" Burt said. He turned to the waitress who was still lingering nearby hoping for some recognition from Eustace. "How about another?" he asked her, snapping his fingers to get her attention.

Reluctantly the server took his glass and went to the bar. By this point the four sat in silence sipping their cocktails. Ada staring adoringly at *HER* husband, Joann glaring at Burt, and Burt glaring at Eustace who looked as relaxed as can be.

"So Burt, the editing, how is it going?" Eustace asked again, sitting back in his chair.

"The students are handling that, so I imagine it'll be a disaster." Burt said, thinking about the hack jobs and out of focus features the students had produced for their mid-term project a few months back.

"Oh I'm sure it's going to be wonderful," Joann chimed in looking back at Eustace. She had never noticed before, but underneath all that tweed his body looked really solid, like something she could climb on and ride for hours. Joann licked her lips.

"Hungry, darling?" Burt asked her.

"Yes, yes I am," Joann said without taking her eyes from Eustace. Eustace assessed her then turned his attention to Ada.

"Have you decided what to order?" he asked her. Ada was busy running her foot up Eustace's pant leg. How jealous would Joann be if Ada just slipped under the table? She suddenly felt sexy and out of control, younger than she'd ever felt. Without even trying to be discreet, Ada knocked her butter knife off the table with an elbow.

"Oops, how clumsy," Ada said, sliding from her chair to the ground.

Burt rolled his eyes at the scene, thankful the waitress just put a fresh drink in front of him. "Just keep 'em coming," he told the woman.

"Are you ready to order?" The waitress asked, thinking maybe the fourth member of the party was just in the ladies room and not groping her husband under the table.

"Lamb with mint sauce for my wife. A steak for me, rare, if it's not too much trouble," Eustace said.

"No, of course not." The waitress said, turning to leave.

"Hey, what about us?" Joann barked.

The waitress looked at them as if just realizing they were sitting there. "Sorry, what did you want?" she asked.

"The crab," Burt said. "And Jo do you want the chicken or-"

"I want steak, rare, just like what he's having." She gestured to Eustace, almost spilling her sidecar in her lap.

"Good choice." The waitress gave her a knowing look.

Ada meanwhile was on her knees, worshiping the lower half of her husband. "What in the hell is she doing down there?" Joann finally asked, pulling up the tablecloth. "Ada!" She shouted so everyone on the patio turned to look.

Ada was busy trying to get into her husband's pants, who casually sat there sipping his whiskey as if nothing was happening. "Jealous?" Ada asked, pausing a moment to meet Joann's gaze.

"Of what? That you're a whore?" Joann said, laughing. "You little slut." Burt downed the rest of his drink and reached over to finish off Ada's martini. This couldn't be happening.

"Excuse me? What is your problem? If I want to give my husband fellatio what business is it of yours? You didn't seem to mind when I went down on you," Ada said.

"Jo, what the hell is she talking about?" Burt slurred.

Joann sat back, feeling panic bloom red on her cheeks. "Nothing, she's crazy Burt. What is she even talking about? I'm not the one who's a lesbian here." Joann snuffed, taking another drink, trying to forget about Ada's tongue caressing all the right places. It was right before Ada went insane and threw that shoe at Joann's forehead. Jo still couldn't make sense of that afternoon.

"A lesbian? Would a lesbian do *this*?" Ada said, fighting with the zipper on Eustace's trousers while he just chuckled and shrugged at Burt, *Silly women, huh?* he seemed to say. Burt however, did not think any of this was funny.

"Stash, how about you get your wife off her knees, huh? People are trying to eat. This isn't a peep show," Burt finally said.

"Exactly. Thank you." Joann said, splashing the remains of her drink down the front of her dress. "Where's that waitress?" She waved to a server passing by. "Another martini, dirty," she called to him.

"Huh? Okay, I'll go tell Julie," he said.

"Great, you go tell Julie. Tell her to hurry up with my steak while you're at it. I'm eating for two now." Joann yelled.

"Quiet down, you're making a scene," Burt told his wife.

"I am? Look at her," Joann gestured to Ada sitting under the table, her head in Eustace's lap while he caressed her hair like a pet.

"Enough of that. Get the hell up, Ada. Eustace, have some respect." Burt said.

Eustace directed Ada's eyes up to meet his gaze. "Burt is uncomfortable, honey. How about you come back to the table?"

"Ugh, fine. Party poopers." Ada said, crawling out from under the table and back up into her seat. She found her cocktail empty but didn't care. She took Stash's glass from his hand and took a long, slow drink. She watched Joann's eyes cross.

After a still silence, Joann attempted to collect herself, remembering why she was upset to begin with. "My dress, Ada. I want it back."

"Why?" Ada swallowed, feeling the whiskey bite her throat.

"Because it's *my* dress."

"Soon you'll be too fat to wear it anyway. Besides I took the waist and bust in so it probably won't even fit you now, ha!" Ada said, feeling really smug.

"You know what? I've had just about enough."

Joann slammed her glass onto the table. Despite Burt trying to hold her in place, Joann stood up and glared down at Ada. "Now look here." She began thrusting her finger in the air, "Give me back my fucking dress!"

"Jo!" Burt gasped. But Joann twisted away, picking up her glass and throwing the whole thing at Ada.

"You cunt!" Ada screamed. "You're just jealous of me because I have everything! Because I'm free! I'm a better artist. I've got a better husband. I'm from California. My husband is better looking. And we both know I'll be a better mother than you ever will." Ada began trying to unzip the back of the gown. "Here you want it, take it!" she said still struggling to get the thing off.

Joann could only see red, because Ada was right. Her husband *was* better looking than Burt. Eustace made the juices between her thighs drip.

Jo didn't know what she was doing, but she rushed around the table so quickly Burt couldn't have stopped her. She grabbed Ada and began yanking at her hair so both women tumbled to the ground. The half undone gown fell off one shoulder, exposing Ada's silk slip.

Ada grabbed Joann's long pearl necklace and began choking her with it. Joann felt around on the floor for the knife Ada had knocked off earlier. Burt and the other diners looked on in horror as the two women rolled off the patio and onto the nearby grass. The waitress came by and set the plates down, nearly dropping the steak in Eustace's lap as she couldn't take her eyes off the fighting women.

"Sorry," she apologized.

"No need," Eustace said, continuing to slowly sip his drink and watch the scene. Joann began grinding at Ada's hand with the dull blade of the butter knife. Ada howled and threw an elbow into Joann's face.

"They're like two cats huh?" Eustace said to Burt.

"Aren't you going to do something?" Burt asked, getting up. "Help me."

"Help you? Burt, trust me, this may look serious, but it is much healthier this way." Eustace told him. Burt hated that annoying subtle grin that always seemed to sit in Eustace's mouth these days. He wanted to peel it off and smash it under his shoe like a roach. That's what his colleague and former friend reminded him of, a fat, grinning roach.

In the meantime, three of the waitstaff were pulling the women apart. In the end there were cuts, scrapes, bite marks, tousled hair, and ripped gowns. Burt helped Joann to her feet. One of her heels broke so she had to hobble out of the restaurant. "See you on Monday, Burt," Eustace called.

Burt shot him an angry look before turning away. He heard Eustace laughing behind him. "Have a good night you two." Eustace called before turning back to Ada. "Now Ada, what are we going to do with you?"

Ada sat down on her husband's lap. Eustace zipped up the back of her dress. The two shared the steak and had the lamb wrapped up to go.

As the pair ate in the corner of the patio they failed to notice the bothered women who couldn't help but run their hands suggestively over their husbands, or rub their feet against their date's leg under the table.

When Ada and Eustace walked out, the restaurant smelled like a orgy of the damned rather than a club for casual dining. The red glass windows out front made the light look lewd and forbidding.

Ada and Stash passed a number of cars in the parking lot, windows hot with steam, moans coming through the glass. "Love is in the air, isn't it?" Ada laughed, gripping onto her husband's arm.

"It is the breeding season," Eustace said, opening the door of the Bel Air for her.

"Why thank you," she said, sliding in.

Eustace obliged his wife, letting her blow him on the ride home. Then fucked her blind before bed. After she was out for the night, Eustace got up, replaced his clothing and went downstairs to the garage.

The light from the chest freezer illuminated the new Eustace's face as he stared down at the wrapped up pieces of the original doctor. The shadow self felt the organic body of Eustace frozen in time.

The creature was many things, but not one of them was enough to sustain a body for more than a few weeks without a living presence. Already his flesh felt clammy and he was growing paler by the day. If only that nitwit hadn't severed his link to this world by murdering her husband. But he guessed a few weeks was enough to finish the taping.

After that he'd be burnt onto film instead of wandering the hallways of human loneliness waiting for someone to stumble in from the cold.

9.

Eustace walked down the hallway leading to the film studio. He heard the voices of the students arguing about how to cut the introduction.

"We want to keep it simple," Burt's voice filtered in over the talking. "Remember if you cut into the budget for animation or music you'll be lacking somewhere else."

Good old Burt, always the voice of reason, Eustace thought. "Good morning," Eustace said entering the storage room/studio. The crowd of eight students and Burt paused in their discussion.

"Uh, morning," Burt said, trying to remain professional, but the entire weekend all he could think about was the look of indifference on Eustace's face as the wives ripped each other to shreds at the club. He'd known Eustace since the man had moved here, more than a decade ago, and this man didn't seem to be him.

Burt couldn't quite put his finger on it. Physically he looked mostly the same, maybe a little slimmer and better groomed, but it was undoubtedly Eustace and yet… it wasn't. The idea gave Burt the chills.

"Are we ready to get started?" Eustace asked, sitting down in the chair he had the students drag down from his office. It was the nicest thing on set.

At first Eustace was annoyed with the lack of production quality but quickly realized it didn't matter. It was

Him people were going to be focused on, not the background or the lighting.

"We were discussing the opening," one of the students said. A few others groaned.

"What about it?" Eustace asked, sitting down and lighting a cigarette.

"I think animation is the way to go, like the title of the program and maybe a little jingle. But *Thomas* thinks we should have more of a soap opera entrance with-"

"That's not what I said," Thomas interrupted.

"Well that's what I got out of it," the girl shot back. Soon the debate began again with Burt stuck in the middle looking like he wanted to kill them all.

"Everyone, I have a solution," Eustace said, barely raising his voice. The students, much to Burt's surprise, fell silent immediately. "There will be no introduction sequence. Just flip on the camera, display the session number and then we'll go directly into the program. Can you handle that?" Eustace asked as if he were talking to small children.

"But we should at least have some kind of music," one said.

Eustace sighed, people had to complicate everything. "Fine, we'll add a signal bell to the beginning and end, how's that? Simple and clear, that's what I want."

"Sure, got it."

"Minimalism."

"Bells would be pretty neat."

"Yeah, unique."

Burt stood there in disbelief a moment before saying, "So uh, we're all in agreement then? We want this
stripped down from start to finish. No intro or outro?" Burt
clarified. Everyone nodded their heads.

"Wonderful. Can we please get started then? My
time is precious. Oh, and Burt when do you think these will
air? Have you been able to secure a better time slot?" Eustace asked.

"Same time slot, I told you. No one wants to listen
to this mumbo jumbo." Burt was at the end of his rope with
Eustace. He could barely stand to be in the same room as
him.

Since the incident at the club he wanted to be done
with Eustace and Ada as quickly as possible. He didn't
have a clue about how the strange pair found out Jo was
pregnant. She swore up and down she didn't say anything.
Burt could only rationalize that he let it slip into a conversation somewhere and hadn't realized it.

"Burt?" Eustace asked. Burt saw the students and
his former friend staring at him.

"What are we waiting for? Let's get this over with,"
Burt yelled, clapping his hands.

"You're in frame," the woman behind the camera
said.

Burt, embarrassed, rushed off to the side. "Sorry,"
he mumbled. "Whenever you're ready."

The camera focused in on Eustace, but Burt noticed that instead of looking into the lens his friend was smirking at him. It was a subtle knowing smile, as if the bastard were in Burt's head, reading his thoughts right now.

Finally, Eustace looked away and directly into the camera, his face transforming into a soft, understanding doctor.

"Does this look okay?" A student whispered from behind the camera.

"Looks fine," Burt said, walking past. "I need to get some air, but uh, do whatever and let's wrap this up," he said.

He was still outside, smashing his second cigarette butt into the dirt when he heard the heavy door open and bang shut. Burt didn't bother looking over at Eustace, he could feel the man there. That's something else that turned Burt's stomach, the way his former friend's presence felt like a cold wind on a sunny day. He could always feel Eustace nearby, and it felt heavy and empty, leaving you wondering what's changed here? What's missing from this picture? Humanity was the only thing Burt could conclude.

"Eustace." Burt acknowledged before turning to go back inside.

"In a rush?" Eustace asked, pulling a cigarette from his brass case.

"No, I just have to get back is all. You know how it is when you leave students alone."

"I heard you might be moving. That wouldn't be because of girls would it? Because you know how women are."

"I don't see how that's any business of yours. In fact," Burt felt a surge of courage at the moment. He was going to firmly end this friendship. "I think once we're finished with this filming business we should go our separate ways. Obviously things have changed. I don't know how or why, but they have. I can feel it in my bones, something isn't right here," Burt said.

"Careful Burt, you're starting to sound like one of our wives," Eustace teased.

Burt felt himself flushing with anger. He opened his mouth to cuss the man out but a young student running across the green lawn caught his attention. She waved frantically while calling out, "Oh Dr. Gish! Dr. Gish!" She came to an abrupt halt before the two men.

"Good afternoon Sharon, whatever could you possibly need that has you running like that? There's not a devil chasing you is there?" Eustace asked.

"Ha, no, I just had a few things I wanted to fill in. You know, a few gaps in my notes for the upcoming exam."

"I'm sure you could get whatever you need from one of the other students," Dr. Gish replied, sounding almost bored. He exhaled smoke in the girl's face, but she didn't react. A wide smile was plastered on her face, and she appeared to be sweating.

"No, Dr. Gish, they can't help me," she said, in all seriousness. She gave Burt a side eye as if he were intruding on a personal conversation.

Eustace took a second to look at her, threads of panic were appearing around her eyes. Finally, he tossed his cigarette on the ground and smashed it with his polished shoe. The flat look on the man's face lifted and he grinned, "Well then, how about we go to my office?" He turned to Burt, "No rest for the wicked."

Burt continued to watch his former friend and the student, Sharon. Now that he really looked, the girl seemed on edge about something, almost as if she were fighting to repress her tremors. Her hands were grasped so tight he saw her knuckles turning white. It reminded him of Joann when she was taking Obetrol.

Whatever was going on Burt didn't want any part of it. "See you tomorrow, same time," Burt said, pushing the filming schedule forward as much as he was able. If he students weren't such whiny fuck-ups and had some actual teeth he'd have them film several in one day. But knowing them they'd get the reels mixed up and cut the wrong things together, making a clusterfuck of the whole thing. Then they'd have to start over, prolonging the entire unpleasant experience.

Eustace might have said something, but it was brief. The doctor's full attention was on the student. Burt paused in the doorway, watching. Eustace had put his arm around the girl's shoulder, he was leaning in and whispering as the pair walked away in the direction of his office.

"What the hell is going on?" Burt wondered out

loud. His friend seemed to be replaced with a pod person, yet everyone was too blind to notice. In fact, when they got home from the restaurant the other night, despite all that had happened, all Joann could talk about was Eustace and how good he was looking lately.

"I can't believe he's even still married to Ada," Joann rambled. "He's way too good for that loony. That's why they made divorce, to get away from women like that. I mean, really, how does he ever expect to rise through the ranks with her at his side?"

She ran on and on, even when they were in bed. Finally Burt couldn't take it anymore and told her to shut it. After that they laid in the darkness, both thinking very different thoughts about Eustace.

"Do you want to have sex?" Joann asked after ten minutes of silence.

"No," Burt snapped. He was usually never one to turn down sex with his hot young wife, but his libido was killed by all this talk of his friend.

"What do you think about that eye? I don't know… You'd think it would make a person look ugly or handicapped, but somehow he makes it look… kinda mysterious. Don't you think so?" Joann commented.

"Jo!" Burt roared, throwing back the blankets and getting out of bed.

"Burt, where are you going?" she asked, even though it sounded as if she could care less.

"I'm sleeping in the guest room. I'm tired of hearing

about fucking Eustace. As far as I'm concerned you're all insane." Burt slammed the door.

Over the weekend the couple barely spoke. And now, seeing Eustace walking away with that student, Burt had a compulsion to step in, run over there, and pull the girl away. But he stopped himself, *she's an adult not a child. She's not being kidnapped. Whatever is going on is their business,* he told himself.

+++

Ada didn't bother to drive since Joann's house was only a short walk. She carried the emerald dress folded over her arm like a used dish towel. Ada had to get her business in order.

Obviously Joann and Burt were toxic, and Ada wanted all of those negative vibes out of her life. She had begun reading the hardbound edition of *A Familiar Face* that Eustace had given her. She could tell she'd grown spiritually since Eustace burned her last copy, because it made a lot more sense now.

Plus it helped that Ada was more committed, and Eustace actually believed in the process now. She could talk to him about it and he advised her on how to translate the ancient wisdom into everyday practice.

Today she was taking action to bring her vision of the future into being. Her first step was to rid herself of Joann, this included her ugly dress. Ada had no idea what she was thinking when she took it. But there was no point wondering about it now, that was the old her. Now she had a clear path with a supportive husband.

Ada pressed the doorbell. When no one answered she buzzed it again and again, finally leaving her finger on the button until Joann threw open the door.

Despite it being afternoon Joann was in her house frock with her hair pulled up in a messy bun. She looked green. "Ada, now what? I'm sick, please just go," Joann said. She'd been vomiting since she was five weeks but it seemed to be getting worse. She was losing instead of gaining weight. Her beautiful plump cheeks looked skeletal and her healthy glow had turned into a waxy sheet.

"I'm just bringing your dress back. I don't know how it ended up in my closet, but if you're going to be that dramatic about it as to attack me then here, take it." Ada tossed the dress into Joann's arms.

Joann examined the garment, looking at the long tears down the front. It seemed as if someone had gone to town on it with a pair of scissors. "Ada, what the hell is wrong with you?" she gasped. "Why would you-"

Ada cut her off, "Careful Jo, you should embrace your pregnancy because it can be taken away just like *that*." Ada snapped her fingers. "No one likes a whiny baby." She looked Joann over one more time as if she were disgusted.

Beneath the thin house dress Ada could see the plump womb rising. She ached to reach out and pluck it but restrained herself, knowing it wasn't ripe yet.

"Get out of here, you're crazy!" Joann screamed, throwing the shredded dress on the porch before slamming the door.

Ha, who looks crazy now, Ada thought as she walked away. She wasn't the one leaving clothing all over the lawn and shouting at neighbors in broad daylight.

Ada stopped home to grab her car. Her next stop was to visit the art department at the university. The head of the department, Martin Byrd, had been to a few of their cocktail parties. He also owned a small gallery in Old Town. Ada was sure once she told him about her work and had him over to the house he'd give her a show.

Ada braced herself as she pulled into the parking lot outside of the large tan building. This was how it began. Right now she was just a regular housewife but soon she'd be thrust into the national spotlight. *TIME* would be over to do a photo shoot with her probably within months of her debut. Ada just hoped she was ready for it.

The hallways were long and quiet at this hour. She'd called and asked Martin if he'd be available. He said to drop by anytime in the afternoon, he was normally free. She found him standing in his classroom frowning at a student trying to apply paper mache to the face of a second student. "Don't move," the woman said, draping paper strips over the other's face.

"Martin!" Ada called, walking in. He turned and took in the woman he vaguely recalled from the few times they'd socialized. She was an anxious bore like the rest of the faculty wives. He much preferred that busty one Burt was married to.

"Aw, Mrs. Gish, it's wonderful to see you again." Martin Byrd put on the professional smile that he used to woo the dean into giving his department more money.

"I hope I haven't caught you at a bad time," she said, noting the student struggling beneath the weight of the suffocating mask.

"Just one more layer. I want it to be sturdy," the girl whined. The other's response was muffled beneath the cast.

"No, it's the perfect time. I don't think I'm needed here anymore. Stephanie? Roger? Remember to clean up when you're finished." Martin was thankful to get away, student art was not only overdone and over thought, but the end result was usually overly boring. They spent so much time trying to make their mark and find their style that they failed to recognize it was impossible to create anything original. It had all been done, but of course if they knew that he'd be out of a job.

"I was surprised to hear from you, Mrs. Gish. So what did you have to talk about?" Martin ushered Ada out into the warm afternoon. The smell of cut grass blew in on the wind.

"Well," Ada began, "As I mentioned on the phone, I've been painting and really think it's time to take my work to the next level."

"Oh?" Martin indicated they should sit on the bench beneath the oaks.

"I am very excited about it. And Eustace has been very supportive, which is always a blessing. I took this painting class and I've been studying the wisdom of Swami Nhincomhpoda, plus using Stash's new methods to really guide me through the creative process. So I really think that's transformed my work." Ada went on.

"That sounds great Mrs. Gish-"

"Ada, please call me Ada," she interrupted.

"*Ada*, that all sounds great, but what do you need from me?" Martin asked, knowing where this was heading.

"Well, with my most recent project finishing up, I was thinking about where I would like to make my debut in the art world? So naturally, I thought of you and your gallery." Her smile was too large for her face. Martin could see bundles of nerves collected at the corners of her eyes.

"Mrs. Gish, Ada, that's very thoughtful to think of me. But as you can imagine, it's a small gallery and I have very little wall space at the moment. Besides, I haven't even seen any of your work. And to be frank, I didn't even know you painted," he said.

"I knew you'd say that," Ada shot, barely letting Martin finish his thought. "That's why I'd like to have you and Mrs. Byrd over for drinks."

Martin shifted his weight and crossed his legs, "How many pieces did you say were done?"

"Almost one, but it's a large one. A wall mural done in charcoal, acrylics, some oils, and a few pastels and some markers." Ada said, trying to think of everything she used on the piece. She didn't dare mention her dead husband's blood, though it was her favorite. "And besides brushes I also wanted to make it feel more organic so I used my fingers plus things around the house for texture. You know cotton swabs, basting brushes, combs, just anything I thought could add some dimension to it. It's really something. But I can't take all the credit. Without the guidance of Stash I never would have been able to see what was right there in front of me."

"Uh-huh," Martin said, unsure where to go from there. "Well, with only one piece I'm afraid there's nothing I can really offer. You didn't happen to bring a snapshot of your work?" he asked.

Ada sat there stunned and confused that he wasn't as excited as she was. "Why no… I'm afraid I didn't. And you don't have to worry about gallery space," she hurried.

"Oh, and why is that?" Martin asked.

"Because it's painted on my studio wall. So I thought we could co-host a sort of opening and bring everyone to the house instead," Ada continued smiling, shaking her head, so sure it would all work out.

"I see." Martin sat there trying to think of the nicest

possible way to get off this bench without offending a colleague's wife. "I'm afraid at this time Ada I just don't have the space to fit you in. With classes and a summer student show already planned, I don't have much room on my plate for anything else. Perhaps come back and see me when you've gotten a few more, *smaller* pieces available?"

"But if you could just come-"

Martin looked at his watch, standing up, "It was good catching up with you Mrs. Gish, Ada. I'll make sure to tell Gail you said hello," Martin rushed, giving Ada little time to protest.

"Oh, um, well sure. That sounds grand."

"Good afternoon," Martin said, heading towards the cafeteria. He figured he could still catch a quick lunch if he hurried, but Ada was keeping up with his unnaturally quick pace.

"But what about drinks? You could at least see my work. Maybe one of the students would be interested in writing an article about it for the campus paper?" she tried.

"I'm afraid now is not the best time. We're finishing up our current unit, and things are hectic. I'm sure you understand. But keep working and I wish you all the best," Martin said ducking through the doors of the nearest building.

Ada stood there, frustrated. She took a cigarette out of her purse and tried to light it. "Oh shoot," she said, trying to shake the tremors from her hand to keep the lighter steady. She felt defeated, her art career was ending before it had even begun. She sat back down on the bench, watching the slanting sun stain the warm sidewalk.

"Ada?"

"Huh?" Ada looked up at the sound of her name. "Burt? Jesus, what time is it?" She asked, noticing the shadows had grown long. How long had she been sitting there? Her cigarette had burned down and was cold. She flicked the ash onto the grass.

"Ada, are you alright?" Burt sat down close, maybe a little too close. She wasn't sure if it was real concern or pity on his face, but in the moment it didn't matter. "Burt, I failed, I failed." Ada began to cry out of nowhere, as if her feelings had finally reached their boiling point. "I've failed at everything! I'll never make it as an artist. My womb will never produce a living child. And I hate being a housewife!" she sobbed into his shoulder.

"There, there, you're fine. Where's Eustace?" Burt asked, looking around for the slippery snake.

"How would I know? He goes out at all hours and never tells me anything. He never even sleeps in the bed anymore, just stays up all night working. Oh Burt, what's happened to me? How did all of these worms get into my brain?" Between crying uncontrollably and having her face pressed into Burt's blazer he could only make out every other word.

"Have you read any of the book yet? Is it as good as Eustace says it is?" Burt asked, curious. He'd been working on this show but everyone was kinda winging it.

Eustace had failed to provide an outline, a script, notes of any sort.

Burt was getting the feeling more and more that this whole six step realization thing was bullshit. He stood there and watched Eustace talking into the camera, and it did nothing to make him feel better. If anything, the sound of the guy's voice pissed him off. The only reason he didn't put a stop to the whole thing was because after he raised the issue the first time the four females in the class cornered him, making him swear he'd let them finish. "I will go straight to the dean!" one threatened.

"This is my DREAM project, Professor Milton, *please*, no!"

"You can't stop us from filming, you just can't."

"Yeah, you can't just give us something like this and yank it away." The girls began sobbing and pulling at their hair, much like Ada was doing now. Burt didn't get it. He looked over at the male students in his class and they seemed as dumbfounded as he did.

"Ladies, alright, *alright*, you win. Do what you want, it's your grade. Just get it done." Burt trailed off. All four females exhaled heavy sighs of relief, with one, Katherine, breaking out into gleeful laughter.

Burt looked at Ada, he soothed her hair. Despite everything that had happened between her and Joann, he always thought Ada was okay, a little kooky, but a decent woman where it counted. Now seeing her breaking down on this bench, Burt had to wonder what the hell was going on.

"Stash says I don't need to see the book, that I have him, which is better. He caught me reading one of the drafts and was really upset. But he gave me a new copy of *A Familiar Face*, a hardcover edition. You saw it at the restaurant, didn't you?"

"I think so," Burt said. "The night was so hectic it's hard to remember. So you haven't read his book?"

"No, Burt. Stash says it's more effective if he guides me verbally step by step, so I don't get confused. Why?"

"No reason…" Burt trailed off. "Would you like a ride home, Ada?" he asked. "It's getting late. Eustace will probably wonder where you are."

Ada began to cry again. "He's going to be so annoyed with me. I failed. I was going to become an artist, a real something that he could be proud of. I thought for sure Martin would be excited to show my work, but he wasn't even interested."

"Martin Byrd? I don't think you should put much stock into what that twink thinks."

Ada lifted her head and looked at him, "Really?"

"Of course," Burt handed her the handkerchief from his jacket pocket. Ada blotted her face. "Have you seen that man's painting? Plus his whole gallery is filled with bad student art. I think you'd be better off keeping art as a hobby, and focusing on other career goals."

"Really? Like what?" Ada asked.

"I don't know, hm… I think you'd make a perfectly

wonderful secretary." Burt said.

"I hate talking on the phone to strangers. It gives me hives," Ada told him.

"How about a cashier? They need a new girl down at the hardware store after that uh, horrible accident. Did you hear about that? The owner came around the corner at a hundred miles an hour and mowed the poor girl down."

"How dreadful," Ada said. "Did he do it on purpose?"

"Let's hope not." Burt laughed. "Well, I better get home before Jo sends out a search party. Did you need a ride?" Burt asked, standing.

Ada folded the handkerchief and handed it back to him. Burt tucked it into his jacket pocket as they walked. "That's very sweet of you, but no. I have the Bel Air." Burt walked Ada to her car and watched her climb in and drive off.

The campus was quiet as evening set in. Burt liked this time of year. Classes were ending, students were going home, and the campus became nearly empty. He enjoyed walking the grounds on the warm summer nights.

As Burt turned to head towards his own car, he noticed a figure standing back in the growing shadows of the oaks. He had to stop and look, thinking how strange it was, but why he couldn't say. As if the figure standing there was somehow darker than the shadows around it, more like a rip or hole than a solid person.

The man began to approach, moving along the

path swiftly towards Burt. As he drew closer Burt realized it was Eustace, or more like something wearing Eustace's face. It had a stilted, unnatural walk as it approached.

His neighbor put up his hand to wave, "Burt!" he finally called as Burt turned and walked quickly towards his car. "Stop a moment. Hey, buddy," came an unfamiliar voice from the familiar face. It sounded more like a moist croak, deeper, grittier in contrast to the normal, smooth tone of Eustace. Burt jumped into his car and slammed the door, locking it.

Eustace stopped, standing on the edge of the parking lot. When Burt flicked his beams on they highlighted the man who almost seemed to ripple, more like a reflection than a person. "Gotta get home," Burt yelled through a crack in his window. He put the Buick in reverse and pulled out, watching his headlamps slowly wash over the figure before casting it back into black. Eustace put up his hand to wave, but his face was flat.

Once on the road, Burt pressed the accelerator to the floor, feeling something was chasing him. Finally turning into his driveway, then pulling into the garage, he sat still in his vehicle waiting for the automatic door to close behind him.

Burt kept his gaze forward, waiting until the door was completely shut before getting out. He couldn't bring himself to look in his rear view mirror, afraid the cold sweat of dread that was rapidly spreading over his skin like mildew would manifest a figure he didn't want to see.

10.

Eustace skipped class the next day. He spent most of the morning with Ada, murmuring into her ear to calm her. The phone rang and rang late into the afternoon. "Who keeps calling?" Ada would sniff now and again.

"It doesn't matter. What matters is you. You're not doubting that little bird inside your belly, are you? If you don't take charge, Ada, and do the work you'll never come together."

"Who cares." Ada blew her nose loudly, a snot bubble popping. Large heavy bags had grown under her eyes overnight. Her nose was red, while the rest of her was pale. She reeked of cigarettes, booze, and self doubt.

"Ada, you're still so blind."

The phone rang again. Both Eustace and Ada looked at it. "Ignore that. It's just the outside calling, trying to confuse your mind." Eustace assured her.

"They've been calling all day. Maybe I should answer it," Ada said. Lumbering towards the doorway, her foot caught on the curved leg of the coffee table sending her tumbling to the floor. "Great blazes in Hell!" Ada cried, going down, splashing her drink and soaking the carpet.

"I'll answer it, honey," Eustace said, pulling Ada to her feet and placing her back on the sofa like a doll. "Sit tight, I'll only be but a minute." Eustace went to the kitchen and picked up the phone. "Gish residence," he said.

After a minute there was a voice on the other end. She sounded faded and confused. "Dr. Gish? Dr. Gish, is that really you?" Then it broke into a wailing cry, "Dr. Gish why haven't you answered the phone? I need to see you, please, *please…*" It was that woman from his class, Sharon.

"What is it you need? I thought we straightened all this out yesterday?" he said, voice smooth as honey and just as sticky.

The girl felt trapped, because on one hand she knew he was right - they had just spoken yesterday afternoon. But on the other hand, she had this compulsion to see him, talk to him further and it just would not leave her. It buzzed in her head, unrelenting as house flies banging against a window before rain.

"I just need to see you. I can't… I feel like my thoughts are on fire. I've done everything you told me, all the steps, but…"

"Sharon, I believe you are capable enough to overcome these worries on your own. I am here for you, but sometimes we must tread our paths alone."

"That's bullshit, Dr. Gish!" Sharon shouted. Even she was surprised by her aggression. "I'm sorry." Her voice quickly fell to a whisper, "But Dr. Gish."

Ada walked into the kitchen, staring at her husband on the phone. "I'll be in my office tomorrow and we'll discuss this further. Do not call again." Eustace said, hanging up the phone.

"Stash, who was that?" Ada asked. She braced herself against the doorway. It felt as if the tiles were turning to
iced over puddles, and she couldn't keep her stocking feet
from slipping and sliding all over.

"Ada, how about you turn your energy to your work
hm?" Eustace said, not so much avoiding her question as
simply ignoring it.

"My w-work?" she stuttered. Eustace took her arm
and gently guided her into the dining room/studio, placing
her before the floor-to-ceiling mural she had been working
on for close to two months. He just needed a few minutes
alone from these needy women.

"Oh my work," she said, then began to cry.

Eustace rubbed his face in irritation. "What's wrong
now, *honey*?"

Ada stopped as if someone had turned a dial. "Why
do you always call me that lately?" she asked.

"Call you what?" Eustace just wanted to go into his
study, close the door, and stare out the window at the lake
in silence.

"Honey. It's always *honey this* or *honey that!* Who
are you?*"*

Eustace swallowed his annoyance with the woman.
"Your piece looks as if it's almost finished." Eustace gestured to the mess before them. There were so many layers of paint now that it all blurred into a mass of brown and
sickly olive green. The portrait of Stash, hidden beneath
layers upon layers of oils, acrylics, smears of mud

Ada turned back to the wall, "I am close. At least it feels that way. It's my higher self that will say when it's truly done." Almost with something like reluctance, Ada dragged herself to the small tray table where she kept her brushes soaking in paint thinner. She ran her fingers along the tubes of oil colors. Her touch lingered over blue before moving on. She mixed a sickly pale green with white and began to work. "Maybe I'll add some highlights," she said.

"There, don't you feel better already?" Eustace said, but Ada failed to answer. "That's good, you just work, honey." Eustace said, walking out of the room.

As Ada painted she couldn't help but think of Joann and that baby forming inside of her. The thought of these cells sticking together to create a brand new body fascinated her. Why wouldn't her body do that? All she had was a bird, worms and who knows what else was in there. What did Joann have inside that made her so much better at making a baby than Ada?

Ada dropped the green brush and picked up a new one, mixing a fresh palette of reds. She found great fun at flinging the paint at the wall, watching it splat and run down the bumpy surface in gory rivulets, finally pooling on the floor.

"What do you have inside there, Jo?!" Ada slung more paint at the wall, enjoying the mix of the crimson, pink, and burgundy. "That's my baby. Mine!"

After she grew satisfied with what she saw, Ada discarded her palette, wandering away to make herself a drink. Upstairs she slumped down in the tub, a white Russian in hand, though it was more Russian than white these days. Her hands and the front of her dress were marked with various hues of red. She held out her fingers and examined the spots and streaks drying, vibrant and delicious. "Joann, Joann, Joann…" She sang to herself.

Ada went to set her glass on the edge of the bathtub but missed. The clear tumbler shattered on the floor leaking white Russian all over the torn up surface. "Oops," Ada said, looking over the edge. The mixture flowed among the shattered pieces of mirror that reflected up at her, distorting her appearance.

"My, my, what is going on here…?" Ada trailed off, thinking she looked nothing like herself. It was as if she were seeing herself for the first time - the red marks on her face, the drastic cuts flashing just so that she glimpsed herself from a new angle. She was painted with Joann, saw herself red with Joann's blood, so thick and sticky it dripped from her like syrup.

Ada sat back in the tub after a minute, ruminating on the novel idea of looking inside of Joann as if she were an art exhibit or a creation of grand architecture. Her bone beams and soft pink wall coverings sounded beautiful and exotic.

Perhaps that's why she could grow a baby and Ada couldn't. Ada wasn't soft and warm, but cold and freezer burned. *How depressing,* Ada thought. She reached for her drink but remembered it was broken on the floor, so instead she licked the semi-dry oil paint from her hands, thinking.

+++

"I hope you plan on doing some useful work today," Eustace said to Ada.

"Of course," she said. Both stared at each other as they ate, neither had bothered to get the newspaper off the porch for the last two weeks. "I saw Joann in the parking lot of the grocery store last week. She was loading all sorts of horrible looking things into her car. It's like she's trying to kill her baby. It was just disgusting," Ada remarked.

"Oh?"

"Yes," Ada went on, barely stopping to take a sip of coffee. "Cleaner, soap flakes, shaving cream, cat food, and tons and tons of toilet tissue. Hardly anything edible at all! But she's getting plumper, so she must be eating *some-thing*. Maybe you should have a talk with Burt."

"You say she's looking fatter?" Eustace asked.

"Hm? Yes. Like a whale." Ada chuckled at the thought of waddling Joann. She always had a body men admired. Now she looked like a lumpy old pillow.

"You're looking thinner than ever," Eustace said.

222

"Why thank you. It's mostly paint."

"You don't say?"

"Well if I'm working, I have to stop and eat, so snacking on paint saves time." Ada said as if it was the most logical thing.

"Definitely don't let anything stop you from self-realizing. Whether it be a person or a sandwich," Eustace said. "So what are your plans today while I'm out?"

"Paint. Then at twelve when Jo goes to get her hair done I thought I'd better take another look around her house and see if it's set up for the baby. You know, I bet she doesn't even have the nursery ready yet. I was always prepared. Remember last time? I had the nursery done before I was even out of my first trimester."

"Yes, it's a shame the child didn't survive." Eustace said, taking his cup and saucer to the sink. "Well, I've got class and then a session late this afternoon. We need to re-shoot a few things, but overall it's coming together beautifully. I know Burt will be happy to have it done. Have a nice day, honey." Eustace kissed his stiff wife. She couldn't bear to move after his remark about her dead child. It hit her like ice.

When the front door shut Ada went to her studio. The portrait of Eustace was complete so she'd moved on to the other wall, painting a mural of a ghostly baby floating out of Joann's stomach tethered by an umbilical cord that looked like a hangman's noose. Now on the third wall Ada had begun a sketch of the last step, her ascending to reach The End.

"It's only a matter of time," she told herself, running a charcoal stick over the smooth mauve wall.

+++

The clock chimed twelve and Ada threw down her brush, finally it was time. For the last two weeks Ada had been visiting Joann's house whenever she knew the woman would be out. At first it was just peeking in the windows, trying to see what was going on in there. Soon Ada saw how easy it was to jiggle the back sliding door. Joann was so careless she didn't even bother to put anything in the track in case of real burglars. This baby would definitely be better off with Ada. Frankly, Ada was surprised Joann and Burt hadn't been murdered in their sleep yet.

Inside the house was silent, Joann's calico cat, Munstead, twisted around Ada's feet as she flipped through the mail left on the kitchen counter.

"What do we have here?" Ada asked, looking over several women's magazines, not one having to do with mothering. It was all diets and dating advice. She finally tossed everything back down, bored. "Some people just aren't capable of evolving," she said. Ada turned to go upstairs, nearly tripping on Munstead.

"Ouch! Stupid cat!" Ada cried, giving the creature a

swift kick. She watched it disappear under the hutch in the corner. Now Ada knew why she and Stash never had a pet, they were annoying, useless companions.

Upstairs Ada found what she was looking for. The smell of fresh paint wafted down the hallway, urging Ada to continue on to the room at the end of the hall.

The normally white walls had recently been done a fresh hue of marigold. "Are you kidding me?" Ada looked around inspecting the furniture. It was all dark wood. The whole room was dark. "This is all wrong, all wrong!" Ada shouted. From the dirty yellow walls to the walnut crib, all wrong. "It's supposed to be beautiful!" She began frantically ripping the flowery drapes from the window, tearing the linen off the crib mattress.

After five minutes of destruction the woman sank to the floor of the ruined nursery. She cried, cradling a plaid baby blanket. The fabric was so scratchy, how could Joann even think to wrap such a precious gift in it? "Why, Jo, why?" Ada wept.

She cursed her former friend, but also cried for the baby and herself. Why had she come to this place? Wouldn't she have been better off not knowing the horrors Joann and Burt were going to inflict on that innocent little life? It was like they didn't even care.

Soon Ada's sorrow gave way to a simmering rage. She looked up when she felt something rubbing against her. *Munstead,* she thought, watching at the cat infecting the soft toys, the crib sheet, the carpeting, with its filthy paws, and its mangy hair. "Kitty, kitty…Sweet Kitty" Ada said.

"If someone kicked me, you can bet I wouldn't come next time they called. You really are a stupid thing," she said once she'd scooped the cat up in her arms.

As she hugged it harder, the cat began to moan deep in its throat. "No you don't," Ada said, her voice a hushed tone. "I read an article once about a cat lying on a baby's face and suffocating it during its nap." Ada told the tale as she wrapped the cat in the blanket, tighter and tighter.

Munstead began to thrash, but Ada held it firmly on the ground, kneeling on it, pressing the animal into the thick folds of the blanket. She didn't even feel its claws poking through scratching at her knees.

"Just slip away," she told it while the cat continued to fight for its life. Ada figured this was nothing compared to her quarrel with Stash, now that was a mess.

When the pet finally laid still Ada stood back up, carrying the thing over and lying the whole package down in the crib. Hopefully Joann and Burt would get the message that someone was looking out for their baby.

+++

Afterward Ada drove to the grocery store to pick up dinner. She wandered among the vegetables, then the deli, feeling overwhelmed. There were so many choices…

"Good afternoon, Mrs. Gish," Niles behind the meat counter said as she passed. Ada barely heard him, but gave a dazed wave and continued on. He wasn't surprised. Everyone knew the woman was troubled. She'd been looking more and more unraveled in the last few weeks or so. The man continued watching her, noticing her wrinkled dress, the deep scratches on her hands and dried blood crusted just below her knee. "Mrs, Gish," he went quickly after her.

When she felt a hand on her shoulder she turned, "Hm?" she asked, looking around.

"Are you okay? What happened?" he asked, motioning to her wounded hands, ripped legs.

"What?" Ada turned her hands over examining them. Then she perked up and smiled, "Oh this? It's just paint. I was painting this morning," she said.

"Uh-huh. Are you sure?" Niles could clearly see the marks on her hands were long red scratches. "It looks like you got into a fight with a cat," he said, trying to keep things light, but failing to hide his concern.

"Ha-ha. No, nothing like that. I've just been spring cleaning, you know how it goes. Now I really must excuse myself. I'm running late and have a ton to do," she told the butcher. "Have a nice day."

Niles noticed her smile was large. So large her lips

looked curled backwards over her teeth, it unnerved him.

"Sure, okay Mrs. Gish. I uh, don't want to keep you…" he trailed off watching the woman float off down the nearest aisle as if she didn't have a care in the world.

But Ada did have a care, many cares. She cared about her painting career, about ascending to that higher spiritual plane, about that poor baby. But also about Joann whom she saw wandering at the other end of the aisle only moments before Ada ducked into this one.

Ada wanted to flee the store, but something stopped her. Why was she the one running? Joann was the horrible one. First bullying Ada and making up lies about her, then creating that horrible room for that poor un-born child. Ada bet Joann would probably hire a nanny.

Carefully, Ada edged her cart forwards, peering around the end of aisle five, searching for the woman. If only she could get over to the freezer section she'd just load the cart with TV dinners and get the hell out of there. She really didn't want a scene with crazy Jo today. "Ada?" Ada practically gave herself whiplash turning around.

"Jo?" Ada didn't have to act surprised when she saw her neighbor behind her, because she was. "Where did you come from?" she asked, certain she'd see Joann go down aisle three just moments ago.

"What are you doing lurking at the end of aisles? Think you saw your husband again?" Joann's laugh re-minded Ada of a braying ass. Instead of saying anything Ada whipped her cart around, smashing it into Joann's

228

cart, knocking her back a few steps.

"Ada! Are you crazy?" Joann examined her convex midsection for damage.

"Please, I'd be doing that baby a favor." Ada said.

"Excuse me?" Joann's eyes bugged out of her head. Timid, nervous Ada seemed to be loosing her mind and not in a fun let's-run-off-and-be-lesbians type of way. But in a serious, deranged type of way.

"You heard me. And for all I know you're here looking for *my* husband. Yeah, that's right. I saw the way you were ogling him at dinner a few weeks ago. I know you're jealous. But guess what? He thinks you're disgusting!" Ada really enjoyed watching the emotions flicker across Joann's face.

"You're insane," Joann finally said, spinning on her heels and waddling in the other direction. She noticed the red lines, the scrapes, on her former-friend's skin, plus the paint stains on her once nice dress, but Joann just couldn't care anymore. Ada was obviously beyond help. She had to just focus on Burt and the baby, and try to forget about her old friend and her delicious, sexy husband.

Joan was sure that eventually Stash would come to his senses and come sweeping in to ravage her. She whistled the rest of the way through the grocery store, picking up a head of lettuce, a pound of ham, thinking about that lovely man down the street.

Meanwhile, Ada stood in the freezer section dumping assorted TV dinners into the shopping cart, feeling glum. She paid, rolled her cart out to the Bel Air, and tossed everything through the open passenger side window. As she was pulling out she saw Joann's wide rear end loading her groceries. Ada slowed down, idling just behind the woman. Joann noticed her as she pushed her cart aside and climbed into her vehicle. But Ada remained parked behind Joann's Cadillac.

Finally losing patience Joann laid on her car horn, causing other shoppers in the lot to pause and watch the scene. Ada continued to stare straight forward, car parked. "Ada! Ada! Move your damn car now!" Joann cursed out her window.

Ada continued to focus, her vision narrowing until she was looking down a tunnel. She was sure she saw The End in sight if she looked hard enough. How long until she got there?

"Mrs. Gish? Are you alright?" she heard coming through her window.

"Sweet Jesus, what now?" she asked, cranking down the glass.

"Do you need something?" It looked like the man from the hardware store.

"No, why?" she snapped.

"Well, you see your car is parked-" he was interrupted by the blare of horns. Now a few cars were backed up behind her.

"All this noise, I can't think." Ada reached over and opened the nearest TV dinner, removing the frozen square of applesauce to suck on. Maybe she was just hungry. She'd only eaten paint for the last two days. That's why her brain was so fuzzy. What was she doing at the store again? She had plenty of meat at home.

"Mrs Gish, would you like me to call your husband?" The man offered.

"If I said no, would you hit me with your car like you did that poor college girl?" Ada remarked, tossing the block of the frozen applesauce out her window and speeding off, leaving the man speechless.

+++

The class sat in silence going over their exam. Eustace sat at his desk. He plucked a fresh piece of strudel from a pink box one of his students had so thoughtfully brought for him. "I made it myself. It's a family recipe. My grandmother was from Austria," she'd said, blushing when he examined the treat.

"Aw, absolutely delightful," he smiled, taking the box from the girl. She glided back to her seat aware of the jealous faces around her.

Eustace noticed Sharon was absent, as he assumed she would be. Her new fiancé wanted her to drop out, but she wanted to continue. She was torn and confused so Eustace took her to his office to straighten her out. He didn't expect to see her again. So when Sharon came banging through the doors of the lecture hall twenty minutes before the end of class, Eustace was anything but pleased to see her.

The commotion caused the students to look up from their exams, but the girl's appearance kept them staring. "Dr. Gish!" She screamed from the middle of the steps in the center row.

"Sharon, do you not see that others are trying to take a test? Please, keep your voice down," he told her, somewhat annoyed.

He was filming his final session tomorrow. Things were falling apart, he was ready to move on to a more permanent state of being on film.

"Look at me!" she screamed. Now people were really looking, realizing Sharon's dress wasn't covered with rose blossoms, but with fresh gore. "I did... I did this for you, and now you won't even look at me!" she shouted, pulling at her hair, spinning around as if the whole situation was unbelievable. This couldn't be her life, this couldn't be.

"Sharon-" a boy tried to say but quickly fell silent when Sharon pulled a pistol from her purse.

"Pat bought me this to keep me safe." She sounded sad about it. "He never liked me walking home so late after work, so he got me this," she said, almost tenderly. Sharon cradled the fat firearm in her delicate fingers.

The lecture hall had become a tense diorama of frozen students, a bored professor munching strudel, and this frenzied young woman with a Browning in her hands.

"Now Sharon, there's really no need for the dramatics. How about you go home and let the rest of us interested in learning finish the class, hm?" Eustace suggested, as if it were the most logical thing to do.

"I can't go home. Not after…" she said, finally looking from the gun to Eustace. "I don't want to. I've done everything. Everything! I'm ready, Dr. Gish."

Her look of confusion and madness were swept away by a soft smile, as if she just realized something deeply profound. Sharon felt sure, really sure, she was done. "I love you Dr. Gish!" Sharon said. Without hesitation, she stuck the pistol behind her ear, aimed it upwards and shot on a single round.

Her body fell limp, tumbling down the second half of the stairs to rest in front of Eustace's desk, an offering to him. Eustace stood up, looking at the body, he guessed he'd have to eat the rest of the strudel later.

"Everyone," he tried to say but hysteria had overtaken the student body and most were fleeing. No one dared approach Sharon's body to see if by some miracle she was still alive.

Eustace walked over to the classroom phone and dialed the front desk, informing the secretary of the situation. "Please get yourself under control Mrs. Levine and call emergency services. Yes, lecture hall 36, thank you."

Eustace hung up the phone, tucked the desert under his arm and stepped over Sharon. It was better this way. She was free now.

+++

It was past eight by the time Eustace arrived home. He managed to eat the rest of his strudel on the way so he wouldn't have to share with Ada. He threw the box into the bushes before going inside.

"Stash! Where have you been?" Ada ran to him. "I had the worst day!" she cried, pulling at his jacket.

"There, there, honey. I'm sure it was fine." he said, feeling drained. "How about we-" Eustace was interrupted by banging on the front door just behind him.

"You insane sonofabitch open this door! I saw you go in there. Now open up!"

"What does Burt want?" Ada asked, looking from her husband to the door. She'd all but forgotten about the afternoon innocent with Munstead. "Oh…"

"What did you do now, Ada?" Eustace moved his wife back a few steps before opening the door. He put on a happy grin.

"Burt! What brings you over so late?" Eustace asked.

"What the hell do you think?"

Eustace looked around as if trying to think, "I haven't a clue. We just saw each other at the taping, so what do we possibly have to talk about?"

"Well, my wife just informed me that we'd been broken into. She is beside herself. Our nursery was destroyed! And Munstead was…" Burt trailed off. "Well, Jo found him strangled to death wrapped up in a blanket in the crib!" Burt was red, his skin glossy with sweat. "Now what the hell am I supposed to do with that?" He looked like he wanted to start crying now.

"Burt," Eustace began. "I just had a troubled young woman end her life in my lecture hall this afternoon, as you very well know. Now you're here burdening me with your minor tragedy. If you had a break-in I suggest you go to the police, not me." Eustace said, getting ready to close the door.

"Why you cocksucker! I don't need to call the cops, I know it was your loony wife!"

Ada gasped, "I was at the grocery store," she said as if this proved anything.

"Yeah, Jo told me about the incident where you rammed a shopping cart in her belly then harassed her in the parking lot. Everyone saw Ada! And what are those? Huh? Explain your hands," Burt said, gesturing to the raw lines that covered Ada's knuckles and wrists.

"I've been painting and cleaning. They were scraped. Is that a crime?" Ada said in a crisp tone.

"That's bullshit!" Burt thrust forward determined to squeeze that woman's neck and force her to confess. "I know you're lying you crazy bitch! What did you do?! Just say it!" he roared.

"Enough, Burt," Eustace said, taking a firm arm and throwing the man out the door. His strength caught Burt off guard. Burt stumbled, nearly face planting on the cobblestone walkway.

"I'd say watch your back, Eustace, but I honestly can't tell which one of you is crazier!" Burt shouted. "Just stay away!" he screamed, before wandering off down the road. Eustace closed the door firmly and turned to his wife.

"Now Ada, what happened? They weren't supposed to know you were keeping an eye on them. And killing a cat in the baby's room, what were you thinking?" Eustace tisked her and directed the woman to the kitchen where they both sat.

"I have dinner for you," Ada said, pushing a plate across the table. The meal was still partly frozen and covered with cling wrap. "It doesn't taste as good as it usually does," she remarked, sticking a fork into the white mound of potatoes.

"You shouldn't be harassing Joann." Eustace said. He pushed the plate aside, still full from eating pastry all afternoon.

"I wasn't, she cornered me. I was merely defending myself. And that stupid cat… I never see the damn thing, ever. Then all the sudden it's there at my feet, following me around, like it's keeping tabs on me. And you should have seen the baby's room! Now that's the real tragedy…" she trailed off, biting down on a frozen green bean. "What's all this talk about a dead girl?" she asked, as if it were simply a second thought.

"Sharon isn't important. The final session was taped today, and I'm very tired," he said.

"Of course, oh gosh, I'm so sorry, Stash. How did it go?" Ada felt horrible that she forgot the program finished today. "When will it be on TV?" she asked.

"Whenever the students finish editing. Probably a few weeks I imagine, unless," he looked at Ada.

"What? Unless what?" she finally asked.

"Unless you upset Burt and Jo so badly that Burt decides to pull the plug on the entire thing, students' grades and our dreams be damned." He sounded almost sad about it.

"No, that can't happen. He wouldn't dare!" Ada declared, slamming her fist into the table, making the plates jump.

"However," Eustace looked up at his wife. "Perhaps there's something else to be done."

"Anything, Stash, I'm ready." Ada said, leaning forward. She gripped his hand in hers. "Jesus, Stash, are you feeling okay? Your hand is like ice." She released it, but the brittle cold of his skin wouldn't leave her.

"I just need to rest, Ada dear. Shall we go to take a bath?" he suggested, slowly standing.

The couple ascended the stairs. Eustace climbed into the dry tub with Ada folding in around him.

"It'll all be okay, won't it Stash?" she asked once they were situated.

"Hush, Ada, it'll all be fine tomorrow," he told her.

Ada relaxed because she knew it was true.

11.

"You're going to work?" Ada asked, watching her husband slip on his blazer despite the warm morning. Ada noticed he never changed his clothes, always the dark slacks, white shirt, glasses, and tweed blazer. He was so efficient. Ada wished she could be more like him. Maybe she would be after she ascended, then worldly things like dresses and make-up would be meaningless.

"I have exams to grade. It's easier to do that in my office. Besides, I want to drop in on the AV students and see how they're coming with the film editing."

"Stash, that's so exciting. I can't wait to see you on TV. Even if I have to stay up till one in the morning, it'll be worth it. I'm so proud of you," she beamed.

Eustace gave her a quick peck on the lips, happy he was finally going to be rid of this woman. "Have a nice day, honey." He gave Ada a quick knowing look before heading out the door. Fog was drifting in off the lake giving the morning a dreamy, surreal feel.

Ada watched her second husband disappear into the heavy white blanket that not even the red rising sun could penetrate. She felt it just then, today was different from all the rest.

Ada closed the door and wandered into the dining room. Her work was complete, there was nothing more for her to do here. She felt light, as if she were floating just outside of her body. She and Stash talked about it all night in the tub, he revealed the final step. The thing to do after all the work had been done. "This will be the easy part," he told her. Ada was nervous at first, but now she knew he was right.

She went upstairs humming to herself. She pulled on her gardening slacks and a button down silk blouse covered with red poppies.

In the mirror, she pulled her hair back into a simple ponytail and left the room without applying makeup. Downstairs she left through the patio door, wandering through the streaks of damp fog across the empty lawns towards Joann's house.

Ada knew Joann liked to sleep late when she could get away with it. So naturally she assumed with the pregnancy Jo would still be in bed. Burt would be heading off to finish up his class. Today was the longest day of the year. It was warm, with the plants stretching out to meet the light.

Briefly before entering Joann's through the patio slider Ada looked at the sun over the water, thinking someday it would burn out and fall into a thousand shards like the mirror in the bathroom. Only strange slices of this world would survive. Ada was glad she was moving on as the silent spring gave away to what would surely be a loud summer.

"Jo," Ada's whisper came sharp through her dreams, waking the woman, who thought it was just a nightmare. Joann moaned and stretched, realizing her arms and legs were bound. "Huh?" she said, opening her eyes. The glare coming through the window made everything bright and washed out but she still recognized Ada's sour face.

"It's time for me to go, Jo," Ada said when she saw Joann's eyes flutter.

"Huh?" Joann said again, still struggling to push away sleep.

"I said it's time to go, but I need my final piece. I can't very well leave it here with you."

"Ada, what are you talking about?" Joann tried to sit up, realizing just then Ada had duck taped her wrists and ankles to the bed frame. "Ada, let me up right now!"

Ada put a piece of tape over the woman's mouth.

"I won't let you ruin this for me, Jo. I just know nothing will ever be complete without that baby. I will never be complete, and if I'm not complete how will I ascend to true bliss? Tell me." Ada waited but stunned Jo simply continued to struggle against her bindings. "That's what I thought, you don't have a clue. So just hold still and let's get this over with," Ada said.

Joann could only scream, the tape stuck over her

lips letting out muffled moans. Her eyes were wide, begging Ada to stop. She shook her head, *no, no, please no…*

But the movement was quick, Ada gripped a heavy kitchen knife in her hand. "If the situation were reversed I'd help you Jo, so stop struggling," Ada said, trying to hold Joann still.

"Jo? You up?" Ada stopped upon hearing the front door slam. "Got halfway to work and figured fuck it, it's been a rough few days. How about we head up to the cabin for the weekend? I'll deal with those students on Monday. Either way I'm sure their project will be a mess, so why waste a perfectly beautiful day in that basement, huh?" Burt laughed. "Jo?" Ada heard his voice coming closer down the hall. Joann struggled fiercely trying to make any noise she could.

"Hush," Ada hissed at her and went to hide under the bed. Damn Burt was going to ruin everything.

"Shit, Jo! Baby, what's happening?" Burt rushed in upon seeing the state of his bound wife. He ripped the tape from her lips. "Jo? Jo? Was it-"

Jo managed to get out, "She's under the bed!"

"Ada?" Burt asked, stepping back and flinging up the bed skirt. "Ada!" he yelled, surprised to see the little mad woman crouched in the dark. He reached down to yank her out but she slashed at him, cutting his lower arm. "Sonofabitch! Ada!" he spun around in time to see her dash out down the hall.

"Call the police, Jo, I'll grab her. She's not twisting

her way out of this one."

"But, Burt, your arm," Joann said, seeing the cut crying with blood.

"I'm fine." Burt pulled a hankie from his pocket and pressed it over the wound. "Call the police," he said again before leaving the room. "Ada!" he called, though he didn't expect her to answer.

With shaking hands Joann dialed the sheriff. She heard feet moving through the house, her husband calling after Ada, telling her it was over, the police were on their way.

Joann fell back in the bed, her head spinning, "What the hell," was all she could say.

"Shh," Ada poked her head in the bedroom door before quickly darting off in the other direction.

"Burt! Burt! She's here! Burt!" Joann shrieked.

"Where?" Burt came rushing in red and huffing.

"I think she went down the back staircase to the kitchen. She's just playing with us, Burt. Stay here until the police come."

"I can't, Jo. What if she hurts someone else? Did you see that knife? Christ, I'm lucky she only got my arm. I don't even want to think…"

"Don't go there, Burt. We'll be fine." Joann assured him.

"Lock the bedroom door after me, okay. If you see the police before I do, tell them everything."

"Okay, Burt, okay." Joann said as her husband left.

She forced her aching body up and clicked over the lock. Hearing the back door slam, Jo rushed to her window to see Ada stumbling over the back lawn towards their boathouse.

Joann ran back to the bedroom door to call for her husband, "She's heading toward the dock!" She screamed.

Joann returned to the window in time to see her husband dashing across the patio and down the gentle incline of their yard, calling for Ada to stop. Joann placed her hand over her belly, Ada might have Stash but Joann had his baby. She felt the thing inside of her kick, as if pleased with the whole situation.

At the end of the dock Joann saw Ada pause and look back towards the house as if she sensed Jo and the baby.

"Ada!" Burt called, slowly approaching the woman.

Ada felt trapped, nothing was going as it was supposed to. She wasn't complete without her baby. Would she still reach The End without the child?

Burt was approaching and Ada felt she only had a few choices. Stab him, and head back to Jo, get the baby and then move on. Or she could simply take her chances and hope for the best as far as uniting with her highest self. Sirens were growing louder and Burt was coming closer, gesturing for Ada to just drop the knife and come with him.

The little bird of fear was pecking at her eyes and Ada thought she saw the light at the end of the tunnel. "Goodbye, Burt. Tell Jo to paint the nursery pink. The baby will like that," she said, sticking the knife into her midsection and pulling upward, before falling backward into the water. Burt heard a sickening wet *smack!* as Ada's head hit the corner of the paddle boat tied nearby.

"Fuck, Ada!" Burt ran to the edge of the water and looked down into the murky black tainted with red clouds that resembled bursting flowers. Burt couldn't believe what just happened. He never in a million years would be able to get that image of Ada out of his head. Her tense face going slack, the way she just let herself fall without a groan or a scream, but serene and calm. How was he ever going to tell Eustace?

+++

"Burt, you're kidding," Joann sat on the sofa, clutching her husband's hand. "In the freezer? But how…?" She trailed off more troubled than Burt even. Her friend was dead, her husband's remains found in the freezer. "I just don't get it," Joann paused and looked at him, "for weeks? But all this time, the tapes and the dinner and…"

"I know, hun, I know. I don't understand it either." Burt tried to comfort his wife, placing a possessive hand on her stomach. "Let's go up to the cabin, huh? By the time we get back on Monday the police will be gone and we can try to heal from this. I'll call Victor and talk to him about putting the house up for sale, how's that?"

Joann sniffed and blotted her face, she was so confused. Stash had been dead for weeks, but both Jo and Burt had talked to him, saw him moving around, and yet the facts didn't lie. Eustace was dismembered and packed in the freezer beside the Bel Air. It appeared to the detective that pieces had been sliced off. They suspected Ada might have been eating him. "Okay, Burt. I'll go pack a bag."

"Sure, take your time. I'll lock up and phone my mother to let her know we're okay."

"What about your students? I thought you were supposed to be working with them today to finish up those, uh, that show…" she trailed off again, not wanting to think about the strange tragedies of Eustace and Ada.

"I'll deal with it on Monday. Give 'em the weekend to finish up. I'll just give them passing grades, and call it a day. But uh, again, let's talk about it on Monday, huh? I've got a headache just thinking about it."

"I hear ya Burt, nothing the cabin and some good cocktails can't cure," Joann patted her husband's knee, and stood up, groaning.

+++

Burt stood in the deserted AV room. It was early so none of the students were there yet. On his desk sat six reels of cut film with a note from one of the girls, "Sandy, Rachel, Debbie, and myself worked all weekend. It's perfect. The guys didn't show up."

Burt picked up the reels and looked them over. He wasn't even curious to see the final result. The thing on that film wasn't his friend Eustace.

Burt didn't want to think too hard about it. So instead, he wandered into the storage room and unlocked a cabinet, dumping the reels into a box on the bottom shelf. As he locked the doors he heard the voices of students coming down the hall.

Epilogue - 1998

"What do you think are on these?" Alicia held up two of the six reels of film. "There's a bunch in here."

"Are they labeled?" Jessica asked.

"No, just numbered. Um, let's see." The girl pawed through the box. "Looks like six all together. Must be a set."

"That film looks like it's going to catch fire if we try to play it. I don't know anything about 35mm. Let's give them to Shawn and see if he can put 'em on DVD. He knows all about the archival type stuff."

"Should we just throw them out?" Alicia looked at Jessica. "It might be nothing."

"What? No way. What if it's like the Zapruder film or something? You know other people were there that day and they've never been able to find any other footage."

Alicia laughed, "Whatever. If you think he'll do it." She handed the box over to her friend. "Put it on the cart then."

Afterward the girls wheeled their findings of an old camera, chemicals, and film reels down the hall to Shawn's workstation.

They left a note asking him to transfer the film to disc so they could watch it. *We'll split the profits if it's valuable,* Jessica wrote. She stopped in the door, "Ali, you coming? What is it?" Her friend was staring down into the box, almost transfixed. "Ali?" Jessica placed a hand on her friend's shoulder, making her jump. "What is it?"

"Hm? Uh, nothing. I just got this image in my head for a second. It was weird, I felt like I was dreaming…" she trailed off.

Jessica pulled the door open. "So I take it the new drugs your therapist has you on aren't working out?"

Alicia shrugged, "Guess not. Guess I'm still crazy."

The girls left, letting the door slam shut behind them.

About the author

Elizabeth Bedlam lives, writes, designs
from Michigan, USA